Chellie stared at him. She said uncertainly, 'Go—with you?' She shook her head. 'I—I don't think so.'

'Listen,' he said. 'And listen well. I may be the first man to pay for your company, but I certainly won't be the last. And the next guy along may not respect your delicate shrinkings. In fact, he could even find them a turn-on,' he added laconically. 'And expect a damned sight more pleasure from you than I've had. Are you prepared for that?'

She was quiet for a moment. 'Why should I trust you?'

'Because you can.'

Sara Craven was born in South Devon, and grew up surrounded by books in a house by the sea. After leaving grammar school she worked as a local journalist, covering everything from flower shows to murders. She started writing for Mills & Boon® in 1975. Apart from writing, her passions include films, music, cooking and eating in good restaurants. She now lives in Somerset. Sara Craven has appeared as a contestant on the Channel Four game show *Fifteen to One*, and is also the latest (and last ever) winner of the Mastermind of Great Britain championship.

Recent titles by the same author:

HIS FORBIDDEN BRIDE
HIS TOKEN BRIDE
THE MARRIAGE TRUCE

THE BEDROOM BARTER

BY

SARA CRAVEN

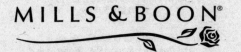

MILLS & BOON®

First published in Great Britain 2003
Harlequin Mills & Boon Limited,
Eton House, 18-24 Paradise Road, Richmond, Surrey TW9 1SR

© Sara Craven 2003

ISBN 0 263 83713 0

Set in Times Roman 10½ on 11 pt.
01-0204-53490

Printed and bound in Spain
by Litografia Rosés, S.A., Barcelona

CHAPTER ONE

THE waterfront was crowded, the air full of the reek of alcohol, greasy food, and the sultry rhythms of local music. People had spilled out of the crowded bars and sleazy clubs, forming shifting and edgy groups in the stifling humidity of the South American night.

Like a powder keg that only needed a spark was Ash Brennan's wry assessment.

He moved easily but with purpose, at a pace barely above a saunter, over the uneven flagstones, his cool blue glance flicking over the gaudy neon signs advertising booze and women, ignoring the glances that came his way, some measuring, some inviting. All the time maintaining his own space.

Logistically it was only about a mile from the Santo Martino marina, where millionaires moored their yachts and where all the nightspots and casinos which catered for well-heeled tourists were sited. In reality it was light years away, and any tourist foolhardy enough to venture down here would need to take to his expensive heels or risk being mugged or worse.

Ash reckoned that he blended sufficiently well. The sun-bleached tips of his dark blond hair brushed the collar of the elderly blue shirt, which lay open at the throat to reveal a tanned muscular chest. Faded khaki pants clung to lean hips and long legs. His feet were thrust into ancient canvas shoes, and a cheap watch encircled his wrist.

His height and the width of his shoulders, as well as his air of self-possession, suggested a man who could take care of himself and, if provoked, would do so.

He looked like a deckhand in need of rest and recreation, but selective about where he found them.

And tonight his choice had apparently fallen on Mama Rita's. He went past the display boards studded with photographs of girls in various stages of undress and down two steps into the club, where he paused, looking round him.

It was the usual sort of place, with a long bar and, closely surrounded by tables with solely male occupants, a small stage lit by powerful spots, with a central pole where the dancers performed.

The air was thick with tobacco smoke and the stink of cheap spirit. And, apart from the sound of the piano being played by a small sad-faced man with a heavy moustache, there was little noise. For the main part, the clientele sat brooding over their drinks.

Waiting for the girls to come on, Ash surmised.

Just inside the door, an enormous woman sat behind a table. Her low-cut sequinned dress in lime-green billowed over her spectacular rolls of fat as if it had been poured there, and her curly hair was dyed a rich mahogany. Her lips were stretched in a crimson-painted smile which never reached eyes that resembled small dark currants sunk into folds of pastry.

Mama Rita, I presume, Ash thought with an inward grimace.

She beckoned to him. 'You pay the cover charge, *querido*.' It was an instruction rather than a question, and Ash complied, his brows lifting faintly at the amount demanded.

'I only want a drink, Mama. I'm not putting in an offer for your club.'

The smile widened. 'You get a drink, my man. My best champagne, and a pretty girl to drink it with you.'

'Just a beer.' Ash met her gaze. 'And I'll decide if I want company.'

For a moment their glances clashed, then she shrugged, sending the sequins rippling and sparkling. 'Anything you say, *querido*.' She snapped her fingers. 'Manuel—find a good table for this beautiful man.'

Manuel, tall, handsome and sullen, set off towards the front row of tables clustering round the stage, but Ash detained him curtly.

'This will do,' he said, taking a seat at the back of the room. Manuel shrugged and went off to the bar while Ash, leaning back in his chair, took more careful stock of his surroundings.

He'd been told that Mama Rita had the pick of all the girls who came to Santo Martino, and it seemed to be true. A few of them were already sitting with customers, encouraging them to run up bar bills of cosmic proportions, but there were several lined up at the bar and Ash surveyed them casually as he took out a pack of thin cheroots and lit one, dropping the empty book of matches into the ashtray.

They were a fairly cosmopolitan mix, he thought. All of them young and most of them pretty.

He spotted a couple of North Americans and a few Europeans, as well as the local *chicas* who'd strayed into port from farms and plantations of looking for an alternative to early marriage and endless childbirth. Well, they'd found that all right, he thought cynically, stifling a brief pang of regret. Because he wasn't there to feel compassion. He couldn't afford it.

'You see something you like, *señor*?' Manuel was back with his beer, his smile knowing.

'Not yet,' Ash returned coolly, tapping the ash from his cheroot. 'When I do, I'll let you know.'

Manuel shrugged. 'As you wish, *señor*. You have only to speak.' He nodded towards an archway with a beaded curtain behind the stage. 'We have rooms—very private rooms—where the girls would dance for you alone,' he added with blatant insinuation. 'I can arrange. At a price, *naturalemente*.'

'You amaze me,' said Ash. 'I'll bear it in mind.'

The beer was surprisingly good, and wonderfully cold,

and he took several long deep swallows, turning his attention away from the flashing smiles of the hopeful girls and focussing instead on the piano player who was still doggedly persisting with a range of old standards in spite of the indifference of his audience.

I hope the old witch at the door pays you well, brother, Ash told him silently as he stubbed out the cheroot. You deserve it.

The pianist reached the end of his set and half-rose to acknowledge the non-existent applause. He seated himself again, and struck a chord loudly.

The bead curtain shivered and admitted a girl.

At her entrance a strange sound like a low growl went through the room. The predators scenting their prey, Ash thought with distaste, then paused, eyes narrowing as he saw her properly.

She was blonde, and slightly less than medium height in spite of her high heels, her slim, taut body complemented by the fluid lines of the brief black dress she was wearing. The strapless bodice was cut straight across the swell of her high rounded breasts, making her skin glow like ivory. The silky fabric clung to her slender hips, ending just below mid-thigh, giving the troubling impression that beneath it she was naked.

But she did not climb up on the stage and begin her routine. Instead, head slightly bent, looking at no one and ignoring the whistles and ribald shouts, she skirted the edge of the platform until she reached the piano. She leaned back against it, as if glad of its support, while the pianist played the introduction to 'Killing Me Softly'.

She had an incredible face, Ash thought frowningly, his attention completely caught. In contrast to the tumble of fair hair on her shoulders her brows and lashes were startlingly dark, fringing eyes as green and wary as a cat's. She had exquisite cheekbones, and her mouth was painted a hot, sexy pink.

And she was scared witless.

He'd known it from the moment of her entrance. Even across the crowd of waiting men he'd felt the force of her fear like a cold hand laid on his shoulder. Now he noticed the small hands balled into fists among the folds of her skirt, the blank, tense smile on her lips.

She was like a small animal, he thought, caught in the headlights of a car and powerless to move.

But there was no problem with her voice when she began to sing. It was low-pitched, powerful and faintly husky. The kind of voice a man would want to hear moaning his name at the moment of climax, Ash thought, his mouth curving in self-contempt.

Her audience was listening while she sang, but with a faint restiveness. However appealing her voice might be, it was the promise offered by the skimpy dress that mattered to them. They couldn't believe it was just a song that was on offer. All the other girls took off their clothes, so why shouldn't she?

She moved effortlessly into the next song—'Someone to Watch Over Me'. She was no longer staring at the floor. Her head was up, and she seemed to be looking far beyond the confines of the club with a wistfulness and undisguised yearning that matched the words of the song.

And in that moment, as her voice trembled into silence, Ash's gaze met hers over the heads of the crowd. Met— and held it for one endless, breathless moment.

Now, he thought, I know why I came here tonight.

The number over, she ducked her head swiftly and shyly in response to the sprinkling of applause, and went back the way she had come. Ash waited to see if she would glance back at him, but she did not, simply vanishing behind the curtain, followed by catcalls and shouts of disappointment.

Ash drained his beer and got to his feet. Mama Rita looked up at his approach, her eyes sharp and shrewd.

'You want something, *querido*?'

'I want the songbird,' Ash said levelly.

She considered that. 'To sit with you—have a few drinks—be nice?'

'Nice, yes,' Ash told her. 'But in one of your private rooms, Mama. I want her to dance for me. Alone.'

Her brows lifted and she began to laugh, the sequins shaking and flashing. 'She's my newest girl. She still learning, *mi corazón*. And maybe I'm saving her for a rich customer, anyway. You couldn't afford her.'

He said softly, 'Try me.'

'Crazy man,' she said. 'Why spend all your money? Choose another girl. One who dances good.'

'No,' he said. 'The songbird. I'll pay the price for her.'

She looked him over. 'You got that sort of money?' There was frank disbelief in her voice.

'You know that I have.' Ash took a billfold from his back pocket, peeled off some notes, and tossed them on to the table in front of her. 'And I know what I want.'

She picked them up swiftly. 'That for me,' she said. 'Commission. You pay her too. Whatever she worth. Whatever you get her to do. Should be easy,' she added. 'Beautiful man like you, *querido*.' She chuckled again. 'Teach her some lessons, *Sí*?'

'*Sí*,' Ash said softly. 'The lessons of a lifetime.' He paused. 'Does she have a name?'

She tucked the money he'd given her into her cleavage and surged to her feet. 'She called Micaela.' She leered triumphantly at him. 'You have another beer—on the house. I go tell your songbird that she's lucky girl.'

I only hope, Ash said silently, watching Mama Rita's departure, that she thinks so too.

But that, he thought as he went back to his table, was in the lap of the gods—like so much else. And he ordered his beer and settled down to wait.

Chellie sank on to the stool in front of the mirror, gripping the edge of the dressing table until the shaking stopped. It was nearly a month since she'd started singing in the club, and she ought to be used to it by now. But she wasn't, and maybe she never would be.

It was the men's faces—the hot, hungry eyes devouring her—that she couldn't handle, the things they called out to her that she was thankful she couldn't understand properly.

'How do you bear it?' she'd asked Jacinta, one of the pole dancers and the only girl working at Mama Rita's to be even marginally friendly.

Jacinta had shrugged. 'I don't see,' she'd replied brusquely. 'I smile, but I don't look at them. I look past—think my own thoughts. Is better that way.'

It seemed wise advice, and Chellie had followed it. Until tonight, that was, when, totally against her will, she'd found herself being drawn almost inexorably to a man's gaze. True, he'd been sitting by himself at one of the rear tables, in itself unusual, as most of the male clientele liked to bunch at the front, baying like wolves for every inch of exposed flesh. But that wasn't the only thing that had seemed to set him apart.

For one thing, he was clearly a European, and they didn't get many at the club.

For another, he was strikingly—almost dangerously attractive, his surface good looks masking a toughness as potent as a clenched fist.

Even across the crowded club he'd made her aware of that.

She thought in bewilderment, Somehow he made me look at him...

So, what could have brought him to seek the tawdry erotic stimulus of a place like Mama Rita's?

Chellie's experience of men was frankly limited, but instinct told her that this was the last man on earth who would need to buy his pleasures.

Oh, God, she thought impatiently, things must be bad if you're starting to fantasise about a customer.

And things were indeed about as bad as they could get. Her life had become a nightmare without end, she realised as she peeled off the loathsome blonde wig, and ran her fingers thankfully through the short feathery spikes of raven hair that it concealed.

Mama Rita had been adamant about that. Brunettes were no novelty in this part of the world. The men who came to her club wanted blondes, and pale-skinned blondes at that.

It had seemed such a small concession at the time, and she'd been so desperate—so grateful for a place to stay and the chance to earn some money—that she'd probably have agreed to anything. Especially as she was being given the chance to sing. She'd thought it was the end of the disasters that had befallen her. Instead, it had only been the beginning.

She wouldn't need to stay at the club long, she'd told herself with supreme confidence. She'd soon save enough for an air ticket out of here.

Only it hadn't worked out like that. The money she received had seemed reasonable when it was first offered, but once Mama Rita had exacted rent for that tiny cockroach-ridden room on the top floor of the club, money for the hire of the tacky dresses she insisted that Chellie wore, and payment for the services of Gomez the piano player—which she was convinced he never saw—Chellie barely had enough left to feed herself.

And, worst of all, Mama Rita had taken her passport, which was about all she had left in the world, and locked it away in her desk, making her a virtual prisoner.

The trap had opened and she'd walked straight into it, she realised bitterly.

There was always the option of earning more, of course, as Mama Rita had made clear from the start. Chellie could be friendly, and sit with the customers, encourage them to buy bogus and very expensive champagne. But even if the thought of it hadn't made her flesh crawl she'd been warned off by Jacinta.

'You earn more—she takes more,' the other girl had said with a shrug.

'You sit with a customer one day; you take your clothes off next. Because you don't get out of here unless Mama Rita says so. And she chooses when and where you go. And you ain't served your time yet.'

She'd paused, giving Chellie a level look. 'There are worse places than this, believe it. And don't try running away, because she always finds you, and then you will be sorrier than you ever dreamed.'

I think I've already reached that point, Chellie thought bleakly. And who ever said blondes had more fun?

She sighed, then got up and began to root along the dress rail in the corner. She performed two sets each evening and had to wear something different for every appearance, which presented its own problems. When she'd begun, she'd worn evening dresses, but these had gradually been taken away and replaced by the kind of revealing costumes the dancers and hostesses wore. Which severely restricted her choice.

She bit her lip hard when she came to the latest addition, a micro-skirt in shiny black leather topped by a bodice that was simply a network of small black beads. She might as well wear nothing at all, but she supposed that was the point Mama Rita was making.

But that's never going to happen, she told herself with grim determination. I'm going to get away from here somehow, whatever the risk. And from now on I'm trusting no one. Especially men...

Her whole body winced as she thought of Ramon. She tried very hard not to think of him, but that wasn't always possible, although the physical memory of him was mercifully fading with every day that passed. She could barely recall what he looked like, or the sound of his voice. One day she might forget his touch, she thought with a shiver, or even the painful delusion that she'd been in love with him.

In a way, she acknowledged, everything that had occurred between them seemed remote—as if it had happened to two other people in some separate lifetime.

Only it hadn't, of course. And that was why she found herself here, duped, robbed and dumped, in this appalling mess.

It might be humiliating to retrace the steps that had brought her here, but it was also salutary.

After all, she'd needed to escape from her life in England and the future that was being so inexorably planned for her. In spite of everything, she still believed that. It was just unfortunate that, through Ramon, all she'd done was jump out of the frying pan into a fire like the flames of hell.

But somehow she was going to wrench her life back into her own control.

I'll survive, she told herself with renewed determination.

As she hung the black dress back on the rail the flimsy curtain over the dressing room entrance was pushed aside and Lina, one of the lap dancers, came in.

'Mama Rita wants to see you, girl, in her office—now.'

Chellie's brows snapped together. It was the first time she'd been summoned like this. Usually a girl was called up because of some misdemeanour, she thought, tensing in spite of herself. She'd seen several of the girls with scratched faces and bruised and bleeding mouths after an encounter with Mama Rita's plump ring-laden hands.

Aware that the dancers operated a grapevine second to none, she strove to keep her voice level. 'Do you know why?'

Lina's eyes glinted with malice. 'Maybe you're going to start working for your living, honey, like the rest of us.'

Chellie faced her, lifting her chin. 'I do work—as a singer.'

'Yeah?' Lina's tone was derisive. 'Well, all that may be about to change. The word is that some guy wants to know you better.'

Chellie felt the colour drain from her face. 'No,' she said hoarsely. 'That's not possible.'

'Take it up with Mama Rita.' Lina shrugged indifferently. 'And don't keep her waiting.'

The office was one floor up, via a rickety iron staircase. Chellie approached it slowly, the beat of her heart like a trip-hammer. Surely—*surely* this couldn't be happening, she thought. Surely Lina was just being malicious. Because Mama Rita had told her at the beginning that there were plenty of willing girls at the club, and that she would never be pressured into anything she did not want.

And Chellie had believed that. In fact, she'd counted on it.

There was a clatter of feet on the stairs and Manuel came into view.

Chellie stepped back to allow him to pass, trying not to shrink too visibly. From the moment she'd started working at the club she'd found him a problem. If she hadn't already been repelled by his coarse good looks, then his constant attempts to get her into corners and fondle her would have aroused her disgust.

The first night in her cramped and musty room, some instinct had prompted her to wedge a chair under the handle of her door. And some time in the small hours she'd woken from an uneasy sleep to hear a stealthy noise outside, and the sound of the handle being tried in vain. She'd observed the same precaution ever since.

There was no point in complaining to Mama Rita either, because the other girls reckoned Manuel was her nephew—some even said her son.

Now, he favoured her with his usual leer. '*Hola*, honey girl.'

'Good evening.' Chellie kept her tone curt, and his unpleasant grin widened.

'Oh, you're so high—so proud, *chica*. Too good for poor Manuel. Maybe tomorrow you sing a different tune.' He licked his lips. 'And you'll sing it for me.'

She controlled her shiver of revulsion. 'Don't hold your breath.'

The office door was open and Mama Rita was sitting at her desk, using her laptop. She greeted Chellie with a genial smile. 'You were a big hit tonight, *hija*. One of the customers liked you so much he wants a private performance.'

Chellie's heart skipped a beat. 'Any particular song?' She sounded more cool than she felt.

'You making a joke with me, *querida*?' The geniality was suddenly in short supply. 'He wants that you dance for him.' The mountainous body mimed grotesquely what was required.

Chellie shook her head. 'I don't dance,' she said, her mouth suddenly dry. 'I—I never have. I don't know how…'

'You have watched the others.' Mama Rita shrugged. 'And he don't want some high-tone ballerina. You have a good body. Use it.'

Yes, Chellie thought, but I've only watched the girls table dancing in the club itself. That has limits. The private room thing is totally different…

She said desperately, 'But you employ me as a singer. That was the deal. We have a contract…'

Mama Rita laughed contemptuously. '*Sí*, but the terms just changed.'

'Then you're in breach, and that cancels any agreement between us.' Chellie kept her hands bunched in the folds of her skirt to conceal the fact that they were trembling. 'So, if you'll return my passport, I'll leave at once,' she added with attempted insouciance.

'You think it that simple?' The older woman shook her head almost sorrowfully. 'You dream, *hija*.'

'I fail to see what's so complicated.' Chellie lifted her chin. 'Legally, you've broken the association between us. End of story.'

'This my club. I make the law here.' Mama Rita leaned forward, her eyes glittering like her sequins. 'And you go nowhere. Because I keep your passport as security until you pay your debts here.'

Chellie was suddenly very still. 'But the rent—everything is paid in advance.'

Mama Rita sighed gustily. 'Not everything, *chica*. There is your medical bill.'

'Medical bill?' Chellie repeated in total bewilderment. 'What are you talking about?'

There was a tut of reproof. 'You have a short memory. When you first come here I call a doctor to examine you. To check whether you sick with pneumonia.'

Chellie recalled with an inward grimace a small fat man with watery, bloodshot eyes and unpleasantly moist hands, who'd breathed raw alcohol into her face as he bent unsteadily over her.

She said, 'I remember. What of it?'

Mama Rita handed her a sheet of paper. 'See—this is what you owe him.'

Chellie took it numbly, her lips parting in shock as she read the total.

She said hoarsely, 'But he can't ask this. He was only with me for about two minutes—he prescribed none of the stuff listed here—and he was drunk. You know that.'

'I know that you were sick, girl, needing a doctor. And Pedro Alvarez is good man.' She nodded, as if enjoying a private joke. 'Plenty discreet. You may be glad of that one day.'

She paused, studying Chellie with quiet satisfaction. 'But you don't leave owing all this money, *chica*. So, you have to earn to pay it. And this man who wants you has cash to spend. Good-looking *hombre* too.' A laugh shook her, sending the rolls of fat wobbling. 'Be nice—you could make all you need in one night.'

'*No.*' Chellie shook her head almost violently, her arms crossing over her body in an unconsciously defensive gesture. 'I can't. I *won't*. And you can't make me.'

'No?' The small eyes glared at her with sudden malevolence. Mama Rita brought the flat of her hand down hard on the desk. 'I patient with you, *chica*, but no more. You do what you're told—understand?' She sat back, breathing heavily. 'Maybe I give you to Manuel first—let him teach you to be grateful. You want that?'

'No,' Chellie said, her voice barely audible. 'I don't.'

Mama paused. 'Or I send you to my friend Consuela.' She gave a grating laugh. 'She don't ask you to sing or dance.'

Oh, God, Chellie thought, her throat closing in panic as she remembered overheard dressing room gossip. *Not that— anything but that.*

She bent her head defeatedly. 'No,' she said. Then, with difficulty, 'Please…'

'Now you begin think sense.' Mama nodded with satisfaction. 'Lina will take you to room. Then I send him to you.'

Lina was waiting in the passage outside. She gave Chellie a contemptuous grin. 'Joining the real world, honey? After tonight, maybe you won't be looking down your nose at the rest of us.'

'Is that what I did?' Chellie asked numbly. 'I—I'm sorry. I didn't realise.'

Lina looked at her sharply. 'Hey, you're not going to pass out on me, are you? Because Mama would not find that funny.'

'No,' Chellie said, with an effort. 'I'll try and stay conscious.'

'What's the big problem, anyway?' Lina threw open a door at the end of the passage. 'You must've known Mama wasn't running no charity. So, why come here?'

Chellie looked around her, an icy finger tracing her spine. The room, with its heavily shaded lamps, wasn't large, and was totally dominated by a wide crimson couch with heaped cushions that stood against one wall. Music with a slow Latin beat was playing softly, and a bottle of champagne on ice with two glasses waited on a small side table.

She said wearily, 'It wasn't exactly my choice. I was robbed, and I went to the police. One of them said he'd find me a safe place to stay while they traced my money. And this was it.'

'That figures.' Lina shrugged. 'It's how Mama gets a lot of her girls—she pays the police to send her the debris that washes up on the beach.'

Chellie bit her lip. 'Thanks.'

'*De nada.*' Lina walked to the door, then hesitated. 'Look, honey, it's no big deal. Just smile and make like you're enjoying yourself. It's not your first time—right?'

'No.' Chellie tried not think about those few humiliating, uncomfortable nights with Ramon. At the time she'd thought nothing worse could happen to her. How wrong could anyone be? she asked herself with bitter irony.

'If things get heavy there's a panic button under the table,' Lina added. 'But don't press unless you actually need to, or Manuel won't like it. And you really don't want to upset him. He's one of the bad guys.' She fluttered her fingers in mocking farewell. 'So—good luck.'

All the walls were hung with floor-length drapes, so it was impossible to tell where the window was—if it existed at all. And past experience suggested it would be locked and barred even if Chellie could find it—before the client found her.

But she could really do with some fresh air. The atmosphere in the room was heavy, and thick with some musky scent. She began to walk round the edge of the room, her heels sinking into the soft thick carpet, lifting the curtains and finding only blank wall to her increasing frustration.

She wasn't sure of the exact moment when she realised she wasn't alone any longer.

She hadn't heard the door, and the carpet must have muffled the sound of his footsteps. Yet he was there—behind her. Waiting. She knew it as surely as if he'd come across the room and put a hand on her shoulder.

For a moment she felt the breath catch in her throat, then she allowed the curtain she was holding to drop back into place and turned slowly and reluctantly to face him.

And paused, her eyes widening in total incredulity as she recognised him. As she registered all over again, but this time at much closer quarters, the cool, uncompromising good looks—the high-bridged nose, the strong lines of jaw and cheekbones. The face of a man who did not take no for an answer.

He was lounging on the sofa, totally at his ease. There was even a faint smile playing round his firmly sculpted mouth.

She was more frightened than she'd ever been in her life—her whole body shaking—embarrassed to the point of nausea—yet for one moment her overriding emotion was disappointment.

She'd thought he'd strayed into the club by mistake, but she was wrong. He was no better than the whooping, slavering crowd bunched round the stage. And regret sliced at her.

He said softly, '*Buenas noches*, Micaela.'

Her throat muscles were too taut for words, so she ducked her head in a brief, awkward nod of response.

Micaela, she thought. That was her name in this place—her identity. And her shield. If she could just hide behind it, she could perhaps make herself believe that none of this was happening to her. That she was someone altogether different, in another place, just as she did when she sang. And somehow she would be able to—endure…

He was silent for a moment, the cool blue gaze travelling over her so slowly and thoroughly that it made removing her clothes seem almost unnecessary.

Beneath the fragile covering of the black dress Chellie felt her skin tingle and burn under his absorbed scrutiny. She knew she should begin the pretence. Micaela would force her mouth into a smile, but Chellie found it impossible.

Although this was not the worst that could happen to her, and she knew it. Outside this room, in the real world, was the threat of Manuel and the woman Consuela, and all the other unnamed horrors they implied.

She thought, *I must do this. I have no choice…*

His own smile widened a little. He said, 'Aren't you supposed to offer me a drink?'

'Oh—yes.' She moved to the table, stumbling a little in her haste. Glad of a momentary reprieve. 'Would you like some champagne?'

And in her head she heard the echo of another girl—her father's hostess, making sure his guests had all they needed. A girl she had wanted to leave behind.

Beware what you wish for, someone had once told her. Because it might come true.

'Not in the least,' he said. 'But don't let me stop you. You look as if you need it.'

Chellie paused uncertainly. One of the club rules, she knew, was that the champagne was for the client. The girl did not drink alone, if at all.

She slid the bottle back into the melting ice. She said huskily, 'I—I'm not thirsty.'

'That makes two of us,' he said. 'See how much we have in common already?' There was faint mockery in his voice. He looked her over again, almost meditatively, his eyes half closed.

'I know you can sing,' he said. 'So, shall we discover what other talents you possess?' He leaned back against the cushions—a man preparing himself for enjoyment. 'Starting now?' he added gently.

It was not a request, but a demand. She bent her head in acquiescence and came to stand in front of him, just out of reach but no more than that. Then, slowly, she began to move to the beat of the music.

CHAPTER TWO

SHE had not told Mama Rita the truth when she'd said she couldn't dance. Because dancing had been one of her passions in that other, seemingly far-off lifetime.

Then, she'd turned herself deliberately into a party animal, going whenever she could to clubs and discos, losing herself totally in the pounding noise and frenetic rhythms of the music. Using the fevered momentum of her body to exorcise her teeming frustrations over her abortive singing career—as well as all the other limitations that being her father's daughter had imposed on her life.

But this was not the same kind of music at all. This was slow and swaying, and deliberately, infinitely seductive. It wasn't meant to induce forgetfulness. It had the opposite purpose—to entice the man watching her into opening his wallet to pay for each further revelation.

And that was what she had to do in order to survive.

She tried desperately to remember what Jacinta had told her. Smile, but don't look. Raise a mental barricade and keep the greedy, leering eyes at bay. Close yourself off emotionally from all that follows.

Because this is not you, she reminded herself. This is Micaela, and she does not even exist, so that nothing that happens to her can harm you.

Not that the client's meditative blue gaze held any real hint of incipient lust, or even particular interest in her performance so far. He, too, seemed to be thinking about something else.

He asked for me, Chellie thought, bewildered. So why isn't he looking at me? Am I boring him? Oh, God, I need—

22

I really need to get this right, or Mama Rita will make me suffer.

She began to move her hips with deliberate sinuousness, her hand smoothing the brief silky skirt against her slender thighs, even pulling it up slightly, then letting it drift back. And saw his brows lift in almost mocking acknowledgement of the teasing promise that her actions implied.

'Why not come a little closer?' he invited softly. 'Or does that cost extra?'

Chellie shook her head, not trusting her voice.

'There's nothing to be scared of,' he went on. 'I don't bite, unless specifically requested to do so. And, anyway, I believe the rules state that I'm only allowed to watch—not touch.'

Rules? Chellie thought wildly. In a place like this? What rules could possibly apply? Was he crazy or just naïve?

'Or not without your permission, at least,' he added almost idly. 'Which I admit doesn't seem likely at the moment.' He took out his billfold. 'Perhaps this might soften your heart—hmm?'

He extracted some notes and placed them on the table beside the ice bucket. 'So, maybe we could—move the performance on a little? Just so that my evening isn't completely wasted.'

In other words, he was telling her to take off her dress.

Chellie's stomach lurched in swift panic as she remembered how little she was wearing beneath it. She was braless, and the rest of her underwear was little more than a glorified G-string. Which he would undoubtedly want her to remove as well.

It occurred to her that this stranger would be only the second man to see her naked. The first, of course, had been Ramon, but he'd been in too great a hurry to pay much attention.

Her whole body shivered as she recalled how he'd pushed her back on the bed, the weight of his body crushing her into the mattress, the painful, grunting thrusts which she'd thought would never end.

Which she was going to have to endure again...

He said, 'I'm waiting for you—Micaela.'

If he'd seemed uninterested before, he was certainly giving her his undivided attention now, his mouth oddly hard, the blue eyes implacable, almost analytical—as if he was observing her through a microscope and did not much care for what he saw.

She pivoted slowly in front of him, letting the skirt swing out away from her slim legs. Going blindly, automatically through the motions, while her mind shivered on the edge of chaos.

Oh, God, she thought imploringly. Let this not be happening to me. Let me wake up soon—please...

The zip that fastened her dress was at the side, reaching from breast to hip. Once she began to lower it the dress would simply fall away from her body. And after that there could be no retreat.

Her shaking fingers undid the tiny hook first, then fumbled for the metal tongue of the zip.

And halted as her entire being froze in outrage and rebellion over what she was being made to do. Her eyes met his in a glance that mingled pleading with outright defiance.

She said hoarsely, 'I can't. I'm sorry, but I just—can't...'

She sank down on to the carpet, because her legs would no longer support her, and covered her face with her hands.

She was expecting an angry reaction and knew that it would be perfectly justified. He might even be violent. Or he could just walk to the door and summon Mama Rita— or even Manuel. Her teeth bruised her lower lip as she recognised the kind of retribution she was inviting.

Yet, strangely, it made no difference to her decision, she realised with an odd calm. Whatever kind of aftershock it might create, she knew she could not strip in front of this man or any other.

Nor could she—or would she—allow him any of the intimacies his money gave him the right to demand.

She thought, I'd rather die…

Although death might not be the worst thing that could happen to her.

The silence in the room seemed endless. Perhaps he'd simply walked out already, leaving as quietly as he'd arrived, she thought, venturing to look up. Gone to make his complaint and demand his refund.

But he was still there, lounging on the sofa, apparently unmoved by her outburst. And if he was furious with disappointment and thwarted desire then he was masking it well.

When at last he did speak, he had the gall to sound faintly amused.

'Have you ever considered changing your job?' he asked. 'Because you seem to lack total commitment to your current career.'

Somehow she managed to scramble to her feet, glaring at him as she did so.

She said thickly, 'Don't you laugh. Don't you dare laugh at me—you bastard.'

He stood too. He was tall. Even in her heels Chellie found she had to look up at him, and resented it.

He said with sudden harshness, 'You're right. This is no laughing matter. And it might be better not to call me names.' He gestured at the sofa. 'Sit down.'

'No.' She took a step backwards, hugging herself defensively.

'Do as you're told,' he said curtly. 'Before you fall down again.' He reached into a back pocket and produced a slender hip flask. 'Here.' He removed the stopper. 'Drink this.'

Chellie stayed where she was. 'What is it?'

'Brandy,' he said. 'And a damned sight safer than your boss's inferior and possibly drugged champagne.' He paused, surveying her pale face and shocked emerald eyes. 'Go on—have some. You need it.'

She shook her head. 'My troubles are just beginning,' she said in a muffled voice. 'Brandy won't cure them.' She swallowed. 'I—I'd better go. Do you want me to send you one of the other girls?'

'If so, I'd have asked for them in the first place,' he returned brusquely. 'But I picked you.'

'I know.' Chellie caught her trembling lower lip in her teeth. 'And I'm sorry. I thought I could do this—I—I really meant to—but…'

'For a moment there, I thought so too.' He slanted a wry smile. 'You almost had me fooled. However, I'm trying to live with the disappointment.'

She stared at him. 'You're saying that you *knew* I wouldn't go through with it?' Her voice shook.

'Of course.' He shrugged. 'Now, sit down and drink some brandy.'

Chellie obeyed reluctantly, her gaze mutinous and suspicious. What was going on here? she asked herself. She'd been bought and paid for. Why didn't he insist that she kept the bargain? And how could be possibly have known that she'd fall at the first hurdle?

The brandy was powerful stuff, and she nearly choked as she swallowed it, but she felt it warming her, thawing the icy core lodged deep inside her.

'Thank you,' she said stiltedly, as she handed back the flask.

He shrugged again. *'De nada.'* He sat down too, but at the opposite end of the sofa, deliberately creating a distance between there. It should have reassured her, but it didn't— because he was still there in her sightline—in her space.

'Tell me something,' he said, after a moment, 'do you suppose this room is bugged in any way?'

She gasped. 'What are you talking about?'

'It surely isn't that hard to comprehend.' He spoke with an edge. 'Does Mama Rita use hidden cameras—microphones? Check what's happening?'

Slowly, Chellie shook her head. 'I don't think so. The other girls would have mentioned it, if so.'

He nodded. 'Good.'

Tinglingly aware of his continuing scrutiny, Chellie tugged ineffectually at her skirt, trying to pull it down over her knees.

She said uncertainly. 'Why are you staring at me?'

'Because I've paid for the privilege,' he said. 'So I may as well take advantage of the time I have left.'

Her lips parted in sheer astonishment. 'That's all you want?' she queried huskily.

'It will do,' he said. 'Unless, of course, you'd like to take something off for me?'

There was a silence, then she said in a small, stifled voice, 'I should have known that—all this was too good to be true. Was the brandy meant to give me Dutch courage?'

He said coolly, 'I was actually hoping that you'd remove that ghastly wig. Or are you going to pretend that it's your natural hair?'

She was startled into a faint giggle. 'No—no, of course it isn't. But Mama Rita insists I wear it.' She pulled the wig off and tossed it on to the floor, running awkward fingers through her dark hair.

'Good,' he approved softly. 'That's an amazing improvement.'

Her face warmed, but she said nothing.

She still didn't understand or trust this *volte face*. And even now her reprieve might only be temporary, she reminded herself. He was only at arm's length. Perhaps he was just lulling her into a false sense of security. Whatever, she could not afford to relax.

A fact apparently not lost on him. He said softly, 'You're like a wire stretched to snapping point.'

Chellie sent him a fulminating glance. 'Does that really surprise you?'

'No,' he said. 'What does puzzle me is how you come to be in this hellhole. I'm sure you'll tell me it's none of my business, but, as a life-choice, it seems a seriously bad move.'

'Choice?' she repeated with stunned disbelief. 'Are you mad?' Her voice rose. 'Do you honestly think that if it had been down to me I'd ever have set foot in a place like this?'

'If that's truly the case,' he drawled, 'why do you stay?'

Her hands gripped each other until they ached. 'Because I can't leave,' she said in a low voice. 'I have no money, no passport, and no other option.'

His brows lifted. 'Were you robbed?'

'Mama Rita took my passport.' Chellie bent her head. 'Someone—someone else had my money. As a result I was turned out of my hotel room, and they kept my luggage.'

She paused. 'I'd been suffering from a virus, anyway, so I wasn't exactly thinking straight.' *Quite apart,* she thought, *from realising that Ramon had walked out on me. Left me broke and stranded.*

But she couldn't afford to think about that—about her sheer criminal stupidity. Or she might break down—lose it completely in front of this stranger.

Instead, she straightened her shoulders. 'I knew I needed to find the British consul pretty urgently,' she went on. 'So I stopped this police car to ask the way.'

'Not very wise,' he said.

'So I found out.' She shivered. 'At first the policeman threatened to jail me for vagrancy. Then he seemed to relent. He said the consul's office was closed for the day, but he'd take me somewhere safe in the meantime.'

She tried to smile. 'I can even remember feeling grateful to him. Only he brought me here, where I've been ever since.'

'Hardly your lucky day.' His voice was expressionless.

'No,' Chellie admitted tautly. 'But I know there are worse places than this, because Mama Rita has already threatened me with them if I don't do as she says. I could have ended up in one of them instead.' *And it could still happen...*

Her voice broke slightly. 'You know—I—I really be-

lieved she was going to let me sing my way out of here.
We had this deal—in writing.' She attempted a laugh. 'How
naïve can you get?'

His tone was dry. 'Mama Rita is a woman who believes
in exploiting all the assets at her disposal.' He paused. 'The
only question is—do you intend to stay here as one of those
assets?'

'You mean—why don't I run away?' Chellie shook her
head. 'With no passport I wouldn't get very far. And she'd
simply find me and bring me back—or hand me over to her
friend Consuela,' she added, shuddering.

He said softly, 'In an ideal world, how far would you like
to run?'

She lifted her chin. 'For preference—to the other side of
the universe.'

He said, 'I can't promise that—but there's always St
Hilaire, instead.'

Her brow creased. 'Where is that? I've never heard of it.'

'Hardly surprising,' he returned. 'It's in the Windward
Islands, and not terribly big. I'm taking a boat there for its
owner.' He paused, giving her a level look. 'You could always go with me.'

Chellie stared at him. She said uncertainly 'Go—with
you?' She shook her head. 'I—I don't think so.'

'Listen,' he said. 'And listen well. I may be the first man
to pay for your company, but I certainly won't be the last.
And the next guy along may not respect your delicate
shrinkings. In fact, he could even find them a turn-on,' he
added laconically. 'And expect a damned sight more pleasure from you than I've had. Are you prepared for that?'

Colour flooded into her face. 'You don't mince your
words.'

'Actually,' he said, 'I'm letting you down lightly.'

She was quiet for a moment. 'Why should I trust you?'

'Because you can.' The blue eyes met hers in a single,
arrogant clash, and Chellie found herself looking away hurriedly, aware of the sudden thud of her heart against her

ribcage. Even if he wasn't here alone with her, she thought, he would still be one of the most disturbing men she had ever encountered.

She lifted her chin. 'I've trusted other people recently. It's been a disaster every time.'

He shrugged. 'Your luck has to change some time,' he said. 'Why not now?'

She hesitated again. 'When you say—go with you…' She paused, her colour deepening. 'What exactly do you mean?'

His mouth curled. 'Listen, songbird, if I really wanted you, I'd have had you by now.' He paused, allowing her to assimilate that. 'The boat has more than one cabin, so you can have all the privacy you want. I'm offering you safe passage to St Hilaire and that's all. There's nothing more. So—take it or leave it.'

She should have been relieved at his reassurance. Instead she was aware of an odd feeling closely resembling pique.

She was angry with herself because of it, which in turn sparked a sudden sharpness in her voice. 'You don't look much like a philanthropist to me.'

'Well, sweetheart,' he said, 'your own appearance is open to misinterpretation—wouldn't you say?'

He seemed to have an answer for everything, she thought with growing resentment.

She said, 'It's just that—I can't pay you—as you must know.'

'Don't worry about it,' he directed lazily. 'I'm sure we can reach some mutually agreeable arrangement.' And, as her lips parted indignantly, he added, 'Can you cook?'

'Yes,' she said swiftly, and on the whole, untruthfully.

'Problem solved, then. You provide three meals a day for Laurent and myself, and you'll have paid for your trip several times over.'

'Laurent?'

'The other crew member. Great bloke, but not gifted in the galley.' He paused. 'Well?'

No, she thought, that's not the word at all. 'Dangerous' comes to mind. But so does 'tempting' at the same time.

She said slowly, 'I—I don't understand. Why should you want to help me? We're total strangers to each other.'

'We share a nationality,' he said. 'We're both a long way from home. And one look tonight told me you were in deep trouble. I thought maybe you might need a helping hand.'

She stared at him. 'Your name isn't Galahad, by any chance?'

'No,' he said. 'Any more than yours is Micaela.'

Chellie bit her lip, once again at a loss. 'I'm still not sure about this…' she began.

He gave a quick, impatient sigh. 'Understand this, darling.' His tone bit. 'I'm not about to force you on board *La Belle Rêve*. And I'm not going to beg you on my knees either. It all depends on how badly you want to get out of your current situation. But I'm sailing tonight, whether you're with me or not.'

He paused. 'So—no more discussion. We're wasting valuable time. I'm the rock. This is the hard place. You have to make the decision, and make it now.'

'And when we get to St Hilaire?' she asked jerkily. 'What then?'

'There'll be other choices to consider,' he said. 'There always are.'

'You forget,' Chellie said. 'I still have no passport, which reduces my options to zero. Unless, of course, St Hilaire has openings for singers,' she added wryly.

He was silent for a moment. 'You say Mama Rita took it from you. Do you know where she keeps it?'

'In her desk—locked in the top right-hand drawer. She showed it to me once.' Chellie bit her lip. 'To convince me she still had it, and therefore still had me. Playing cat and mouse.'

'And the key to her desk? Where's that?'

Chellie grimaced. 'On a long chain round her neck.'

He shuddered. 'Which is where it can definitely remain.' He paused, frowning. 'Where will Mama Rita be now?'

'Down in the club. She'll come up at the end of the night to count the takings, but that's usually the only time. She considers she's one of the features of the place. That people come just to see her.'

'Well,' he said softly, 'she could be right. After all, something brought me here this evening. So let's hope that her ego keeps her right there in front of her admiring public.'

'Why? What are you going to do?' she asked.

'Break into that desk, of course.' His tone was almost casual.

Her jaw dropped. 'Are you crazy?'

'Well, we can hardly take the damned thing with us. People might notice.' He gave her a dispassionate look. 'I'm surprised you haven't tried to get into it yourself.'

His faint note of criticism needled her. 'Because I wouldn't know how,' she said tautly. 'Unlike you, it seems.'

'Merely one of the skills I've acquired along the way.' He shrugged, apparently unfazed. 'For which you should be grateful.' He gave her a questioning look. 'I hope there's a back way out of here?'

'Yes, but that's always locked too, and Manuel has the key.'

'Well, that shouldn't be a serious problem.' He got to his feet, and Chellie rose too.

She said breathlessly, 'You don't know him. He's always hanging round—and he has a knife.'

'I'm sure he has,' he returned with indifference. 'I thought when I saw him that serving drinks couldn't be the entire sum of his talents.'

She said in a low voice, 'It's not funny. He's really dangerous—worse than Mama Rita.'

He said softly, 'But I could be dangerous too, songbird.' He paused. 'And don't say that hasn't already crossed your mind.'

She stared at him, the silence between them crackling like

electricity. He knew how to break open a desk, she thought, and he wasn't scared of knives. Just who was this man—and how soon would she be able to get away from him? And, most of all, how much was it going to cost her? Her throat closed.

She said huskily, 'Perhaps you just seem—the lesser of two evils.'

'Thank you,' he said, his mouth twisting. 'I think. Is Mama Rita's office on this floor, by any chance?'

She nodded. 'Just along the passage. You—you want me to show you?'

'It could save time,' he said. 'Also it might stop me intruding on anyone else's intimate moments. I presume this isn't the only private room?'

'No,' Chellie said. 'But this is reckoned to be the best one. It must have cost you plenty to hire it.'

'Well, don't worry about it,' he said. 'I expect to get my money's worth in due course.' He looked into her startled eyes and grinned. 'All that home cooking,' he explained softly.

He kicked the blonde wig out of sight under the sofa. 'You won't need that again.' He looked her over. 'Do you have other clothes? Because you could change into them while I'm breaking and entering.'

'I haven't very much.' It was humiliating to have to make the admission.

'Then grab a coat from somewhere,' he said. 'We need to make an unobtrusive exit, and you're far too spectacular like that.'

As Chellie went to the door she was crossly aware that her face had warmed.

The passage outside was thankfully deserted, but there was a lot of noise drifting up from the floor below—music with a strident beat, and male voices laughing and cheering.

He said softly, 'Let the good times roll—at least until we're out of here.'

The door of Mama Rita's office was slightly ajar, and the

desk lamp was lit although the room was empty. Apart from the desk there was little other furniture, and most of that, he saw, was junk, with the exception of a nice pair of ornately carved wooden candlesticks standing on a chest against the wall. The air was stale with some cheap incense, and he grimaced faintly.

He said, 'She doesn't seem to worry about being robbed.'

'She doesn't think anyone would dare. Besides, she has a safe for the money.' Chellie pointed to the desk. 'That's the drawer.'

'Then I suggest you leave me to it while you go and change. I'll see you back here in a couple of minutes. And bring the stuff you have on with you,' he added. 'If they believe you're still somewhere on the premises, it will give us extra minutes.'

'Yes, I suppose so.' Chellie hesitated. 'Be—be careful.' Her tone was stilted.

He said softly, 'Why, darling, I didn't know you cared.'

'I don't,' she said with a snap. 'You're my way out of here, that's all. So I don't want anything to go wrong.'

He grinned at her. 'You're all heart.'

She looked back at him icily. 'You said it yourself. The rock and the hard place. That's the choice, but I don't have to like it.'

He shrugged. 'I'm not that keen myself, but there's no time to debate the situation now. We'll talk once the boat has sailed.'

Biting her lip, Chellie left him to it.

Once alone, Ash crossed to the door and listened for a moment before pushing it almost shut. Then he went back to the desk, swiftly unbuttoning his shirt and extracting the flat pouch he had taped to his waist. He chose one of the skeleton keys it contained and opened the drawer that Chellie had indicated.

Inside, lying on the untidy jumble of papers, was a large-bladed knife, businesslike and menacing at the same time.

Ash's lips pursed in a silent whistle. 'Songbird,' he said softly, 'I think you may have underestimated Mama Rita.'

There were several passports in the drawer but only one with the distinctive maroon cover. He opened it, swiftly checking the details with a nod of satisfaction.

So far, so good, he told himself.

He gave the photograph a cursory glance, then paused, studying it more closely. The girl in the picture looked back at him, a faint, almost defiant smile playing about the corners of her mouth, the green eyes cool and candid. And totally unafraid.

His mouth curled cynically. 'But that was then, darling,' he told the photograph. 'How things can change.'

He closed the passport, slipping it into his back pocket, then replaced his keys in their pouch, retaping it to his skin.

He took the knife and used it to force open the other drawers in the desk, scattering their contents all over the floor to give the impression of opportunist theft. Then he closed the top drawer and forced that too, using the tip of the knife to damage the lock.

He felt brief sympathy for the other girls whose passports had been stolen and held against their good behaviour, but there was nothing he could do about that.

Besides, none of them were rich men's daughters.

Only you, songbird, he thought. And you're coming with me, whether you like it or not.

Chellie's heart was racing as she went up to her room, and she made herself breathe deeply and evenly, trying to calm down and be sensible. As she opened the door she braced herself against the usual scuttling noises, her skin crawling with revulsion.

At least on the boat she'd be spared that particular nightmare, she thought, switching on the naked lightbulb which dangled from the ceiling. But vulnerable to plenty of others in its place, an unwanted voice in her head reminded her.

She knew nothing about her rescuer—not even his name.

There was no guarantee that he'd keep any of his side of the bargain. In fact, by trusting him even marginally, she could find herself in a far worse mess.

He looked tough enough, she admitted unwillingly. His body was lean and muscular, with wide shoulders and a strong chest. But then the life he'd chosen—delivering other people's boats, with some petty thieving on the side—was a pretty chancy existence.

Under normal circumstances he was the last man in the world she would ever have turned to for help.

But she couldn't let herself worry about that now. Desperate situations required desperate measures, and she had to get away from this place, whatever the means.

Once I'm out of here, and I have my passport back, I can think again, she told herself with a touch of grimness.

It was amazing the effect that even a whisper of hope could have. After these weeks of fear she was beginning to feel a resurgence of her old spirit. The conviction that her life belonged to her again, and she was back in control.

Swiftly, she stripped off what little she was wearing and put on the underwear—white cotton bra and pants—she'd washed earlier in the day. They still felt damp, but that couldn't be helped. She dragged her one and only tee shirt over her head, and pulled on a brief denim skirt. She stowed the black dress and G string in her canvas shoulder bag, along with her few toiletries and what little money she had left.

Then she took her sandals from the cupboard, banging them together

to dislodge any lurking cockroaches, and slipped them on to her feet.

'Ready to go,' she said, half under her breath.

On her way to the door she caught sight of herself in the piece of broken mirror which hung from a hook on the wall. Once more her hand went involuntarily to her shorn head as she experienced a pang of real pain at the loss.

Her hair, dark and glossy as a raven's wing, had been cut

in a sleek chin-length bob when she'd arrived here, but Mama Rita had ordered it to be chopped off to make more room for the wig. Lina had been given the scissors and had enjoyed her task, while the others laughed and jeered.

I'm barely recognisable, she thought.

But maybe that would be an advantage when the time came to continue her journey—alone.

Think positive, she adjured herself.

After all, that was what she had to aim for—to focus on—to the exclusion of everything else. Taking charge of her own destiny once more.

What had happened with Ramon was a glitch, but no more than that. And she would make damned sure that no other man ever made a fool of her again. Including Sir Galahad downstairs.

Him, perhaps, most of all.

She extinguished the light and went quietly down the rickety steps.

She was halfway along the passage to Mama Rita's room when Manuel came round the corner.

Chellie checked instantly at the sight of him, and he stopped too, his eyes narrowing in suspicion.

'*Hola, chica*,' he said. 'What you doing, huh?'

From some undiscovered depth Chellie found the strength to smile at him. 'I thought I'd go down to the bar for a drink.'

'Where's that *hombre* who hired you?' He was frowning.

'Asleep.' Chellie gave him a long, meaningful look from under her lashes. 'And not much fun any more.'

He looked her over. 'Why you in those clothes? And where your wig? You supposed to be blonde.'

'My dress got torn.' She shrugged casually. 'And that wig is so hot. Surely I don't need it just to buy a beer?'

A slow, unpleasant grin curled his mouth. 'I have beer in my room, *chica*. You want more fun? You have it with me.'

'No.' Chellie took a step backwards, her hand closing on the strap of her bag in an unconsciously defensive gesture.

He noticed at once, his gaze speculative. 'What you got there, *hija*?'

'Nothing,' she denied, lifting her chin. 'And I'm going to have my drink in the bar—without company.'

For a moment he stared at her, then, to her astonishment, she saw him nod in apparent agreement. It was only when he slid to his knees, eyes glazing, then measured his length completely on the wooden floor that she realised who was standing behind him, grasping one of Mama Rita's wooden candlesticks and looking down at his victim with grim pleasure.

She said shakily, 'My God—is he dead?'

'Not him.' Ash stirred the recumbent body with a contemptuous foot. 'I knew what I was doing. He'll have a bad headache when he wakes up, that's all.'

'*All?*' Her laugh cracked in the middle. 'Breaking and entering, and now GBH. What next, I wonder?'

'Well, I can't speak for you.' He went down on one knee, and rifled through the unconscious man's pockets, producing his keyring with a grunt of satisfaction. 'But I plan to get out of here before he's missed.' He got to his feet, his glance challenging. 'I have your passport, so are you coming with me? Or would you rather stay here and accept his next invitation? It may not be as cordial as the last,' he added drily. 'But perhaps you don't care.'

Not just the rock and the hard place, Chellie thought. This was the devil and the deep blue sea, and she was caught between them, as trapped as she'd always been.

And, it seemed, she had to choose the devil…

For now, she told herself, but not for ever. That was the thought she had to cling to. The resolution she had to make.

She felt a small quiver of fear, mixed with a strange excitement, uncurl in the pit of her stomach as she looked back at him, meeting the blue ice of his gaze.

She said lightly, 'What are we waiting for, Galahad? Let's go.'

CHAPTER THREE

THE air outside was warm and so thick she could almost chew it, but Chellie drew it into her lungs as if it was pure oxygen.

She thought, I'm free. And that's the way I'm going to stay. For a moment, she felt tears of sheer relief prick at her eyes, but she fought them back. Because there was no time to cry. Instead she had to make good her escape. Or the first part of it, anyway.

Getting out of the club had been just as nerve-racking as everything that had gone before it. They had dragged Manuel, who had already begun to stir and mutter incoherently, into the office and locked him there with his own keys.

The way to the back door led past the girls' dressing room, so they'd had to waste precious seconds waiting for the coast to be clear. He'd gone first, to unlock the rear door, and had slipped past unseen. But when it had been Chellie's turn she'd found herself catching Jacinta's startled gaze.

She'd made herself smile, and even give a little wave, as if she didn't have a care in the world, but there was no certainty that the other girl wouldn't mention what she'd seen once Chellie's absence had been discovered. In fact, she might not be given a choice, Chellie told herself with a pang.

However, she needed to put space between Mama Rita's and herself and waste no time about it, she thought, breaking into a run.

'Take it easy.' The command was low-voiced but crisp,

and her companion's hand clamped her wrist, bringing her to a breathless halt.

'What are you doing? We need to get out of here. They'll be coming after us…'

'Probably,' he returned. 'So the last thing we want is to draw attention to ourselves. If we run in this heat, we'll be remembered. If we walk, we're just another anonymous couple among hundreds of others. So slow down and try and look as if you want to be with me. And for God's sake stop peering back over your shoulder. Your whole body language is shouting "They're after me",' he added, his tone faintly caustic.

'Oh, please excuse me,' Chellie hit back, heavily sarcastic. 'But the role of fugitive is still rather new to me.'

'Just as well,' he returned, unmoved. 'Hopefully you won't have to play it for long.'

He released his grip on her wrist and clasped her fingers instead, drawing her closer to him, adapting his long stride to her shorter pace. Making it seem, she realised unwillingly, as if they were indeed a pair of lovers with the rest of the night to spend together.

On balance, Chellie thought she preferred a bruised wrist to this implied intimacy. The touch of his hand, the brush of his bare arm against hers was sending a tantalising ripple of awareness through her senses, which, frankly, she didn't need or understand.

Life had taught her to be wary of strangers—to maintain her cool in unfamiliar situations. After all, it had taken a long time for Ramon to get under her guard, until, unluckily, she'd taken his persistence for devotion rather than greed.

But now she'd been thrown into the company of this stranger. Condemned, it seemed, to endure the proximity of a man who had no apparent compunction about committing burglary or hitting over the head anyone who got in his way. And knowing it had been done for her benefit hardly seemed an adequate excuse.

Someone who'd just walked in off the street and apparently felt sufficient compassion to take up her cause, she thought uneasily. And, on the face of it, how likely was that?

Sure, he'd offered her a way out, and she'd taken it. Yet she was risking a hell of a lot to accept his help, and she knew it. Which made her undeniable physical reaction to him all the more inexplicable. But if she was honest she'd been conscious of it—of him—since that first moment in the club when their eyes had met. And she'd found herself unable to look away.

When she was a small child, someone had warned her about wishing for things, in case her wish was granted in a way she did not expect. And Nanny had been quite right, she thought ruefully.

Because only a couple of hours ago Chellie had sung about wanting 'someone to watch over her', and that was precisely what she'd got. And every instinct was warning her that, among so many others, this could be her worst mistake so far.

The sooner I get away from him, the better, she thought, her throat muscles tightening. But that's not going to be so easy. Because I seem to have passed seamlessly from Mama Rita's clutches into his.

Oh, God, how could I have been such a fool? And is it too late to redress the situation somehow?

She drew a breath. 'What did you do with Manuel's keys?'

'Threw them into an open drain.'

'Oh.' She moistened dry lips with the tip of her tongue. 'That's—good.'

'I thought so,' he returned with a touch of dryness.

She looked down at the cobbles. 'This boat we're leaving on—where is it exactly?'

'It's moored at the marina,' he said.

'Isn't that the first place they'll look?'

'I doubt it.'

'Why?'

He shrugged. 'Because they have no reason to connect me with boats.'

'You don't seem very concerned.'

'And you're tying yourself into knots over possibilities,' he retorted.

Chellie subsided into silence again, biting her lip. Then she said, 'My passport—you did find it?'

He sighed. 'I told you so.'

'Then—could I have it, please?'

He gave her a swift sideways glance. 'Thinking of making an independent bid for freedom, songbird?' He shook his head. 'You wouldn't get half a mile.'

Knowing he was right did nothing to improve her temper. Or alleviate the feeling that she was cornered.

'Besides,' he went on, 'like Mama Rita, I feel I need something to guarantee your good behaviour.'

She gasped. 'Are you saying you don't trust me?' she demanded huskily.

'Not as far as I could throw you with one hand, sweetheart.' He paused. 'Any more than you trust me.' He slanted a grin at her. 'Grind your teeth if you like, but I'm still your best bet for getting out of here unscathed, and you know it. And what's a little mutual suspicion between friends?'

'I,' Chellie stated with cool clarity, 'am not your friend.'

He shrugged again. 'Well, my Christmas card list is full anyway.'

'However,' she went on, as if he hadn't spoken, 'I'd still like my passport back.' She paused. 'Please.'

'My God,' he said softly. 'The authentic note of the autocrat. That didn't take long to emerge. From downtrodden victim to "she who must be obeyed" in one easy step.' His voice hardened. 'And what am I supposed to do now, darling? Turn pale and grovel? You should have tried it with Manuel. He'd have been most impressed.'

'How dare you.' Her voice shook.

They had stopped walking. Suddenly Chellie found herself being propelled across the quayside and into the shadows between two wooden buildings, where he faced her, his eyes glittering, his hands gripping her shoulders, immobilising her completely. Making her look back at him.

'Oh, I dare quite easily,' he said. 'Because someone should have stopped you in your tracks a long time ago. And then perhaps you wouldn't need me to get you out of this mess now.'

'I don't need you,' Chellie flung back at him recklessly. 'There'll be other boats. I can find a passage out of here without your questionable assistance.'

'Yes,' he said, grimly. 'But probably not tonight. And that's only one of your problems. Because how long can you afford to wait? How long before word gets round that a girl with eyes like a cat and a bad haircut is trying to leave port and Mama Rita tracks you down?'

He paused. 'And there's the small question of cost,' he went on remorselessly. 'You've no real cash, so are you really prepared to pay the alternative price you might be charged? If so, you could find it a very long voyage.'

'You're vile.' She choked out the words.

'I'm a realist,' he returned implacably. 'Whereas you…' He gave a derisive laugh. 'In spite of everything that's happened, you still haven't learned a bloody thing, have you, sweetheart?'

She said in a stifled voice, 'Please—please let go of me.'

'Afraid I might want to teach you a valuable lesson?' He shook his head derisively. 'Not a chance, sweetheart. You're not my type.'

But he made no attempt to release her, and Chellie, trapped between the hard male warmth of his body and the wall of rough planking behind her, felt herself begin to tremble inside.

Suddenly the world had shrunk to this dark corner, and the paler oval of his face looking down at her. The sheer physical nearness of him.

She was dimly aware of other things too. Men's voices shouting angrily and the loud blare of a vehicle horn. But all that seemed to be happening in another world—another universe that had no relevance to her or the quiver of need that was growing and intensifying within her.

She saw his head turn sharply, heard him swear quietly and succinctly under his breath, then, before she could even contemplate resistance, he swooped down on her, and for one startled, breathless moment her mouth was crushed under his.

But not in anything that could be recognised as a kiss. That was the real shock of it all. Because the tight-lipped pressure of his mouth on hers was simply that—physical contact without an atom of desire or sensuality.

A harsh, untender parody of a caress.

And one that was over almost as soon as it had begun.

Chellie leaned back against the wall, her legs barely able to support

her, looking up at him, trying and failing to read his face.

She said in a voice she barely recognised, 'What was— *that* about?'

He said, '*That* was Manuel in a Jeep, with another guy driving him.' He paused. 'Bald, built like a bull. Do you know him?'

'Rico. He's a bouncer at the club.' Chellie spoke numbly, trying to drag together the remnants of her composure without success. 'Did they see us?'

'I think they might have stopped if so,' he said drily. 'Besides, I made sure you were well hidden.'

'Yes,' she said. And, again, 'Yes.' *So that was why...* She shivered.

He took her hand again. 'Come on.'

She hung back, staring up at him, her eyes blank with fright. 'What are we going to do now?' Her voice was barely more than a whisper.

He shrugged. 'We go down to the marina and get aboard the boat, as planned. What else?'

'But—everything's changed.' Her voice was a little wail of protest. 'They'll be there first—waiting for us.'

'Then we'll make damned sure they don't see us.' He sounded appallingly calm. 'But I'd bet any money that they're not going anywhere near the marina. Trust me on that, if nothing else.'

He put his arm round her and set off down the quay again at a brisker pace. 'On the other hand, I'd prefer us not to be loitering around on their return journey. Going on a wild goose chase often brings out the worst in people,' he added wryly.

Chellie went with him mechanically, her thoughts in turmoil. But it wasn't simply the threat of discovery that plagued her. Because, to her own amazement, that no longer seemed to be her first priority.

Instead, she found she was reliving the moment when she'd stood with him in the darkness with his mouth on hers. Examining—analysing every trembling second of it.

And realising, to her horror, that she'd wanted more. That she'd needed him to recognise that she was female to his male. That she—wanted him.

The breath caught in her throat.

My God, she thought, with a touch of hysteria. It's completely crazy. How can I be feeling like this? I—I don't even know his name.

Nevertheless, that was the shaming truth she had to face—to endure. That there'd been more than a moment when she'd actually wanted her lips to part under his, inviting—imploring his deeper and more intimate invasion. When she'd longed to feel his hands on her body—the sting of his thighs against hers.

A soft, aching instant when she'd been ready to go wherever he might lead.

A small sound escaped her, halfway between a laugh and a sob.

He noticed instantly. 'What is it?'

'Nothing,' Chellie disclaimed instantly. 'At least—I—don't think I'm handling this situation very well.'

He was silent for a moment, and when he spoke his voice was abrupt. 'You're doing all right.'

It wasn't what she'd wanted to hear. She'd hardly expected praise of the highest order, but she'd hoped, at least, for a little warmth and reassurance.

She thought, I wanted him to smile at me as if he meant it...

But I mustn't think like that, she told herself in sudden anguish. It isn't right. And it certainly isn't safe.

Although his arm round her felt safe. Safe—but oddly impersonal. Just as his kiss had been.

Well, now she knew the reason for that totally sexless performance. *I made sure you were well hidden.*

Someone to watch over me, she thought wearily. That's what I wanted, so I can hardly complain about the way he does it. And it was only a minute ago, anyway, that he told me I wasn't his type.

She felt her face warm at the memory. She could only be thankful that she hadn't yielded to that swift, burning temptation and responded to the taste of his mouth. Oh, it would have been so frighteningly easy—and such a disaster.

Because he wasn't her type either, she reminded herself forcefully. He was more than merely attractive, and he might have an educated voice, but that was only a veneer. Underneath there was a darkness—a danger.

And certainly no Galahad either, she thought. He was just a buccaneer, like all the others who'd once pursued their predatory trade up and down the Caribbean sea.

If she'd met him in London, or down at Aynsbridge, she wouldn't have given him a second glance.

Unless he'd looked at you first, said a sly voice in her brain. And you'd suddenly found you couldn't tear yourself away...

Her problem was that she wasn't accustomed to instant sexual attraction. Had always written off that kind of emotion as cheap. Told herself that passing attractions could have no place in her life.

Liking should come first, she'd always believed. A mental attunement that could blossom into real love—Shakespeare's 'marriage of true minds' that 'looks on tempests and is never shaken'.

So how, then, did she explain Ramon?

A chapter of accidents, she supposed wearily. She'd been searching desperately for a way to break her father's yoke and release herself from the stultifying boredom of her life. Something that would take her further than non-stop partying.

She had also been rebelling over his persistence in pushing Jeffrey Chilham at her as a future husband. It was to have been a purely dynastic marriage—Jeffrey, a widower at least twenty years her senior, was poised to take over the running of the corporation when Sir Clive retired—and there was nothing the matter with him that a complete personality transplant could not have cured.

He was correct, worthy, and so ponderously indulgent in his attitude to her that she'd often longed to fling herself at him, screaming, and sink her teeth into his jugular vein.

As a result, she'd been driven to parading a succession of totally unsuitable young men in front of her father. She'd had no intention of marrying any of them. She had just wanted to convince Sir Clive that she was a person in her own right, and not for sale. That she was capable of finding her own husband.

Nevertheless, it had been painful to see them fade away, one after the other, after being exposed by him to the social equivalent of an Arctic winter.

The gossip columns had enjoyed a field-day with her, their comments becoming increasingly snide as one relationship after another had withered and died. Chellie had loathed finding herself portrayed as some heartless rich bitch who chewed men up and spat them out, treating love and marriage as a game for her ego.

Ramon had been so different—or was that just what she'd persuaded herself to believe? He was certainly unlike the suits who hung round her, trying to curry favour with her father and failing.

And he'd braved the full force of Sir Clive's icy disapproval to be with her, which had earned him mega-points in her regard at an early stage in their acquaintance.

She'd never dreamed, of course, that she was simply being carefully and ruthlessly targeted.

He'd talked to her, too, in that deep, softly accented voice that seemed to caress her like dark velvet. Shown her for the first time the possibility of another kind of life outside her father's aegis.

He'd spoken to her of rainforests, and rivers as wide as oceans. Of remote *estancias* where herds of cattle grazed on thousands of acres. Of the house that he'd inherited as his father's only son and the fruit and coffee plantations that surrounded it.

And, of course, of the wife he needed to live beside him there. The girl who, miraculously, seemed to be her.

He'd wooed her so delicately, offering her what she'd believed was adoring respect, keeping her newly awakened senses in ferment. She was his angel on a pedestal, to be worshipped always.

He'd sold her a dream, Chellie thought with self-derision, and she'd bought into it completely. She hadn't even thought to ask who was running those vast plantations while he was away. All she could see was herself, riding beside Ramon through an endless sun-drenched landscape. She'd been lost in the glamour of it all.

The question of money had never really been addressed, of course. Ramon was well dressed, had a flat in the right part of town, was seen in the best places and drove a fast car. Naïvely she'd supposed that that, and all his talk of family estates, added up to solvency. And that her own financial standing was immaterial to him.

Boy, was that the mistake of the century, she thought, grimacing inwardly. A little plain speaking on both sides would have saved a multitude of troubles.

And her father's stony opposition had simply fuelled her resolve—her certainty that Ramon, and the life he described so lyrically, was all she would ever want.

And when Sir Clive, working himself into one of his furious rages, had forbidden her to marry Ramon, or even to see him again, the decision to run away with him had almost been made for her.

Perhaps if it hadn't been for his totally unreasonable blanket condemnation of every other man but Jeffrey, she might, in turn, have dealt more rationally with his opposition. Might even have listened to the dossier he'd no doubt had prepared on Ramon and taken his warnings seriously.

Instead, she'd closed her eyes and ears to his outbursts. Ignored his threat to cut her out of his life and render her penniless if she disobeyed him.

Maybe she'd even thought that if he saw her happily married and living a useful, contented life—if there were grandchildren to soften his heart—he would relent and admit he'd been wrong.

In fact, it was supposed to be roses all the way, Chellie thought. But how wrong could anyone be? She sighed faintly.

'Are you all right?' His question sounded abrupt, but the arm around her tightened fractionally.

'Fine.' Chellie forced a smile to reinforce the fib. Remembering how completely Ramon had fooled her had been a painful procedure, but valuable in its way. There was nothing she could do to redeem the past, but the future was a very different matter.

During her time at Mama Rita's she'd found it almost impossible to think beyond one bitter day at a time. Now she had to make serious plans about her life. And, naturally, those did not and could not feature the man walking at her side.

I'll always be grateful to him, she told herself restively. But gratitude is all there can ever be. I don't intend to make an abject fool of myself a second time, however attractive he may be.

She saw with surprise that they'd reached the marina already, and tensed as she looked around her.

Ramon had brought her here, she thought. They'd had dinner at the Casino, then Ramon had played blackjack and lost. She'd ascribed his subsequent moodiness to his bad luck, but she realised now he had been planning his escape—working out how to ditch her and vanish.

Having first given the condemned woman a hearty meal, she thought wryly.

And his scheme had been entirely successful.

She wondered if he'd ever given her a second thought since—concerned himself even marginally with how she might be surviving, alone and penniless, in an alien, dangerous environment. But she doubted it. He probably hoped that she'd simply disappear for good too. And she nearly had.

Her fate had been sealed from the moment he'd discovered that if she married against her father's wishes her trust fund would only become available on her thirty-fifth birthday.

She'd seen the shock on his face when she told him—the total disbelief masking what she now realised had been anger.

But he'd had every right to be angry, she thought with irony. He'd spent a lot of time and effort pursuing a rich heiress only to find, when he caught her, that she didn't have a bean.

That her father had used his money to control her life, refusing to allow her to train for anything which would have allowed her to earn her own living and conceding her only a small allowance.

Pin money, she thought. Isn't that the old-fashioned term? It sounds sufficiently derogatory. Because the only career I was being groomed for was 'rich man's wife'.

And there were plenty of potential bridegrooms right here

in the marina's basin, she realised, with a wry twist of her mouth. There were a lot of glamorous yachts moored there, with some serious partying going on too.

Her ears were assailed by a non-stop barrage of laughter, talk and the chinking of glasses from the floodlit decks. She was dazzled by designer wear and jewellery.

A couple of months ago, if she'd been in Santo Martino, she'd probably have been a guest on one of these boats, working on her tan by day and parading her own wardrobe each evening.

She suddenly wondered what would happen if she walked up one of the gangways and introduced herself. *I'm Clive Greer's daughter, and I need help.*

For a moment the temptation to pull free of her companion's confining arm and make the attempt was almost overwhelming. Almost, but not quite.

My bloody passport, she groaned inwardly. Without it I'm going nowhere, even if they were prepared to lend me a hand. And looking like this, with my hair like a badly mown lawn, would anyone believe me?

She'd already noted and resented some of the disdainful looks being aimed in their direction.

'Come on, songbird. No time for cocktails tonight.' There was a note of amusement in his voice as he urged her forward.

So now he's a mind-reader, she thought crossly.

'People are staring at us,' she muttered.

'Not for much longer,' he returned. 'We'll soon be out of here.'

She bit her lip. 'You haven't seen the Jeep?'

'Relax,' he advised lazily. 'If *we're* getting the beady eye, can you imagine the effect that Manuel and Rico would have on this select gathering? They'd suffer the death of a thousand ice-picks before they'd gone twenty yards.' He paused. 'And there's *La Belle Rêve* at last.'

Chellie's eyes widened incredulously. The motor yacht

was twice as large as she'd imagined, its sleek lines comparing favourably with any of the other boats in the basin.

She said faintly, '*That's* what you're taking to St Hilaire?'

'You don't think I'm capable?' He sounded amused.

'Far from it.' She offered him a swift, glittering smile. 'I suspect you're capable of anything.'

An olive-skinned man with thick curly dark hair, wearing cut-off jeans and a denim waistcoat, was waiting at the top of the gangplank. He watched them come aboard, then looked at her companion, his brows raised, smiling a little.

'*Mon ami*, I was becoming anxious about you, but now I fully understand the reason for your delay.'

He stepped forward, took Chellie's hand, and made a slight bow over it. '*Mademoiselle*, I am Laurent Massim. *Enchanté*. May I know your name?'

Chellie's hesitation was fractional, but it was noticed by the man beside her.

He said with faint amusement, 'According to her passport, she's Michelle Greer, and she's the new ship's cook.'

Chellie bit her lip. Hiding her identity had never been an option, of course, but fortunately he didn't seem to have made any inconvenient connections. But then who would expect the daughter of a major industrialist to be working in a strip club in South America?

Well, she thought, long may he remain in ignorance.

She faced him, chin up. 'And you?' she queried. 'Do you also have a name, or is it a deadly secret?'

'Not at all,' he said. 'I'm Ash Brennan.'

For a moment Chellie thought she detected an odd note in his voice, almost like a challenge. But maybe he was simply responding to her in kind.

He turned to Laurent. 'If we're cleared for departure, I suggest we get going.' He glanced at Chellie. 'And it might be better if you went below before someone realises we're carrying an extra passenger.'

'Thank you.' The adrenalin that had carried her on that

long trek along the quayside had evaporated, leaving her drained and apprehensive.

She negotiated the companionway with care, clinging to the rail because her legs were shaking under her.

She found herself in a large saloon, luxuriously furnished with slate-blue leather seating, expensive rugs on the wooden floor. At one end was a fully stocked bar, and beyond it the galley, streamlined and gleaming like the interior of a spaceship. Chellie regarded it with foreboding.

While she was looking around, Ash joined her.

'We'll be underway very soon.' He studied her with narrowed eyes. 'Are you all right? You don't get seasick, do you?'

She summoned a pallid smile. 'Not as far as I know. And certainly not while I'm still in harbour.'

'The weather report is good,' he said. 'It should be plain sailing to St Hilaire.'

Plain sailing? Chellie controlled the bubble of hysteria threatening to well up inside her. How could it possibly be any such thing?

She shook her head. 'I can't really believe this is happening,' she said huskily. 'At any moment I'm going to wake up and find I'm back in cockroach alley.'

He said quietly, 'It's over, Michelle. Don't you know what this boat is called? *La Belle Rêve*—the beautiful dream. So there'll be no more nightmares.'

She didn't look at him. 'I—I'll try and remember that.'

'You're out on your feet,' he added curtly. 'I'll show you where you're going to sleep.'

She'd half expected to find herself in some tiny cupboard with a bunk, so the spacious stateroom took her breath away. A queen-sized bed, with storage underneath, had been built against one wall, with windows above it. Another wall held fitted cupboards, and there was even her own shower room, compact but beautifully fitted.

She said uncertainly, 'You're sure about this? The owner won't mind?'

Ash shrugged. 'Why should he care? As long as I bring the *Dream* to St Hilaire in one piece.'

He opened the door of one of the cupboards. 'The owner's daughter uses this stateroom when she's aboard. She's left a few of her clothes. Shorts, swimwear—that kind of thing. Feel free to borrow anything you need.'

Chellie gasped. 'I couldn't possibly do that.'

'She's a terrific girl,' he returned. 'She'd want to help, I promise.' He looked her over critically. 'And you're pretty much the same size. Besides, you can't manage with just what you're wearing.'

Chellie looked down at the floor. 'I seem to be beholden to a growing number of people,' she said stiffly.

'Worry about that in the morning,' he returned indifferently. He paused. 'There'll be coffee and sandwiches later, if you're interested.'

'I don't think I can eat a thing.'

'Then I'll leave you in peace.' He gave her a brief, hard smile and turned away. 'Goodnight.'

As the door closed behind him Chellie sat down limply on the edge of the bed. Her heart was beating fast, and she found it hard to collect her thoughts.

Ash Brennan, she said silently. So I know his name at last. But that's all I know. The rest of him is still an enigma. And I mustn't forget that.

However, it seemed that he'd meant what he said. She was just another member of the crew. So maybe her suspicion that she'd merely exchanged one trap for another was completely unfair.

But she couldn't deny that she was in his power, she thought, pressing her fingertips to her aching forehead. Or that she had no real control over how he exercised that power.

His attitude towards her on the way here had been brisk and businesslike, yet she couldn't forget the way he'd watched her in the club when she was singing—or the glittering, unashamed flare of desire in his eyes when she'd danced for him.

But even then he seemed to be wanting me against his will, she acknowledged with bewilderment. And isn't that exactly how I feel myself?

But she was too tired to think straight. Sighing, she rose and went over to the cupboard, examining the clothing that hung on its rail—smart cotton pants and tops, crisp shorts and shirts, and slips of dresses with floating skirts and shoe-string straps, most of them with designer labels. She handled them appreciatively, realising that she and their absent owner were the same size.

In the top drawer she found bikinis and pareus. The second held undies, and nightwear filled the third.

Kneeling, Chellie took out one of the nightdresses, letting the filmy white material drift through her fingers like gossamer. It was enchantingly pretty and unequivocally transparent—d the others were equally revealing.

So this was what the owner's daughter wore during the long, moonlit Caribbean nights, she thought, her mouth twisting a little. But did she wear them for herself alone?

A terrific girl. That was what Ash Brennan had said. And there'd been warmth in his voice—maybe even a hint of tenderness. He must know her very well, perhaps intimately, to make this offer on her behalf. To be so sure she wouldn't mind.

She looked back at the wide bed, wondering if they had ever lain there together, and, if so, why she should care? Especially when she would part from him on St Hilaire, never to meet again.

At the same time she suddenly heard the soft throb of the engine, and realised the boat was moving.

She got to her feet, still holding the nightdress against her.

She said aloud, 'We're on our way. And I'm committed now, whether I wish it or not. There's no turning back.'

And found herself shivering at the stark finality of her own words.

CHAPTER FOUR

HALF an hour later, Ash came down the passageway and paused outside the stateroom door. He knocked lightly, and waited, but there was no reply, and after a moment he opened the door and went quietly in.

He trod silently over to the bed and stood looking down at its occupant, his brows drawn together in a frown. The bedside lamp was still on, so she must have fallen asleep as soon as her head touched the pillow.

She was lying motionless, her breathing soft and regular. Her cheek was cradled on her hand, and the strap of one of Julie's excuses for a nightgown had slipped down from her shoulder, giving her an air of curious vulnerability. Something glistened on her face and, as he bent closer to extinguish the lamp he realised that it was a solitary tear.

His hand lifted, obeying an involuntary impulse to wipe it away, but he managed to control it just in time.

He needed to get a grip, he adjured himself. Next thing he'd be hitching up that errant strap and smoothing those absurd spikes of black hair. Tucking her in for the night, for God's sake. And there was no room for that because, as they said, this was business—not personal.

He switched off the lamp and straightened, leaving just the moonlight flooding through the undrawn curtains.

Chellie stirred suddenly in her sleep, murmuring something, and Ash backed hastily away from the bed, feeling his foot catch against an object on the floor as he did so.

He glanced down and saw that it was her bag, and that the black dress she'd worn at the club was spilling out of it.

He paused, jolted by the sudden memory of how pale her

skin had looked against it, and the smooth, supple movement of her body as she danced for him.

Remembered too that there'd been a moment when he'd let himself forget why he was there. When he'd longed, with an intensity of emotion that had twisted his guts into knots, to see her take it off. When every drop of blood had sung in his veins in anticipation of seeing her naked.

God, he thought with bitter self-derision, just like some adolescent, peeking at top-shelf magazines.

She wasn't the first girl he'd watched take off her clothes, for heaven's sake, but she was certainly the first not to go through with it, he thought, his mouth curling cynically.

And he wasn't the first man she'd stripped for either. He needed to remember that too.

It was no big deal for her, he told himself. It couldn't be, after the way she'd lived her life, so why, suddenly, the maidenly shrinking? Unless she'd balked at being paid to do it.

Whatever the reason, his instinct had told him with total certainty that it wasn't going to happen. And that the desire that pierced him would not be satisfied.

He drew a deep, sharp breath. That, he told himself, had been a moment of weakness that would not be repeated.

He had to ditch those memories—bury them deeply and permanently. Along with the moment when he'd pretended to kiss her, shielding her with his body, and felt her lips tremble under his.

She may be anybody's, he told himself, but she isn't yours. Don't lose sight of that ever again.

He went to the door and left as quietly as he had come.

Laurent was in the pilot house, humming quietly to himself. He looked round as Ash arrived, carrying a plate stacked with chicken sandwiches and two steaming mugs of coffee.

'She is asleep?'

'Out for the count,' Ash confirmed briefly, putting the food down.

'*La pauvre petite*. What an ordeal for her.'

Ash shrugged. 'A self-inflicted wound, but unlikely to leave permanent scarring. She's already showing signs of recovery.'

'You are hard on her, I think.' Laurent took a sandwich and bit into it appreciatively. 'Did you have many problems persuading her to go with you?'

'She was just about to be launched on a career as a lap dancer, and worse. Any alternative would have seemed good.'

'And they just let her go?'

'Not exactly.' Ash smiled thinly. 'There was one hitch, but it was dealt with.'

'I can imagine.' Laurent gave him a wry look. 'They came after you?'

'Oh, they were on our trail. But sadly it was the wrong one. I left an empty matchbook from the Hotel Margarita on the table for them to find, and they went scorching off to the other side of town to browbeat some unfortunate desk clerk.'

'So all is well.' Laurent nodded. 'Victor will be relieved. His faxes are becoming increasingly agitated.'

'Then I'd better put him out of his misery and tell him to keep quiet from now on. As far as the target's concerned, she's just getting a lift to St Hilaire. I don't want anything to arouse her suspicions that there could be more to it than that.'

Laurent tutted in reproof. 'Target! Such a cold word to use about such a beautiful girl.'

Ash's mouth tightened. 'I just want it finished with. I need Daddy to hand over the money for his spoiled princess. One last smooth operation before I retire, and no hiccups.'

'The girl—you think she could make difficulties?'

'Tonight she was so terrified she'd have grasped at any straw she was offered,' Ash said slowly. 'But tomorrow morning she's going to wake up rested and no longer scared stiff. And sooner or later she's going to start thinking, and wondering about things—like how I happened to turn up so conveniently to rescue her. She's going to ask questions.'

'Then let us hope we reach St Hilaire before you have to provide any of the answers,' Laurent said cheerfully. 'Now, go and fax Victor. Reassure him that all has gone according to plan, and tell him to stay off your back.' He shot Ash a shrewd look. 'Then you should also get some sleep, *mon vieux*. Because, if you are right, you could need all your wits about you tomorrow.'

'Later. I'm not tired yet.' Ash took his coffee over to the leather bench and sat down, watching the silvery water rippling past the bows.

Although that wasn't strictly true, he thought. Now that the mission had been accomplished the tension was seeping out of him, leaving him almost boneless with weariness.

But he wasn't going to bed yet, he decided grimly. Not while there was a chance that he was going to lie awake in the moonlight, seeing a girl's dark head on a pillow and the trace of a tear on her cheek. Remembering the fragrance of her skin, and the sweetness of her mouth when he'd held her for that brief time.

He swore under his breath.

It's time you gave up this game, Brennan, he told himself. You're getting soft in your old age. And that won't do. Because it's not over yet, and the stakes are far too high.

And he sighed soundlessly.

Chellie opened heavy eyelids, blinking at the sunlight pouring into the stateroom. For a moment she felt totally disorientated, then as recollection slowly returned she sat up, stretching and running her fingers through her hair.

She was on *La Belle Rêve*, and Santo Martino with all its horrors was far behind her. And for that she was so thankful.

But it was the immediate future that had to concern her now. What would happen when they arrived at St Hilaire? Her options seemed few, and all equally unattractive.

And the last thing she wanted was to find herself stranded and broke all over again in some other remote spot.

She knelt up on the bed and looked out of the window. There was nothing outside but the vivid unbroken blue of the Caribbean as far as the eye could see.

She had no idea what time it was. Ramon had helped himself to her platinum watch along with everything else, and at the club day and night had seemed to merge into a blur. But the position of the sun told her that she had been asleep for a long time, and it was probably time she put in an appearance on deck.

It was so wonderful to have a proper shower again, she discovered gratefully. To feel the sheer bliss of warm water streaming over her hair and body, and to be able to cherish her skin with scented soap and lotions.

If she only had her own clothes to wear life would be almost perfect. As it was, she had no choice but to borrow once more from the owner's daughter.

I'll use the absolute minimum, she thought. And replace every single item as soon as I get the opportunity.

Whenever that will be, she added, biting her lip.

She put on a pair of white cut-offs and a sleeveless jade-green top, thrusting her feet into her own sandals, then, with a certain reluctance, left the stateroom and climbed up the companionway.

She felt frankly awkward about confronting her saviour in the unrelenting light of day. However grateful she might feel, there were inherent difficulties in being under an obligation to a man about whom she knew so little. And to whom she'd found herself so instantly and unwillingly attracted.

Although why she should feel drawn to him she really didn't know. He might have come to her aid when she was in deep trouble, but he hadn't shown her any real sympathy or concern.

In fact, he'd hustled her almost curtly through the streets

and on board this boat, as if he was already regretting the impulse which had led to her rescue.

If impulse was what it had been, she thought, and paused, frowning, at the top of the companionway, aware of a sudden uneasiness.

'So there you are,' said Ash, appearing from nowhere. He was wearing a pair of elderly navy shorts and the rest of him was tanned skin, she realised with a totally unwelcome flicker of excitement.

'Good morning,' Chellie returned coolly. Excitement notwithstanding, he could do with a lesson in politeness.

'Only just.' Unsmilingly he consulted his watch. 'And breakfast is well overdue.'

'I—lost my watch,' she said. 'And I overslept.'

'I'll give you an alarm clock.' He paused. 'You'll find ham in the fridge. We'll have it with scrambled eggs, toast and strong coffee. And sooner rather than later, if that's all right,' he added pointedly.

Oh, God, Chellie thought, her heart sinking. She'd forgotten this particular detail.

She said, 'Scrambled eggs?'

'That's what I said. Is there some problem?'

'Not at all.' Chellie lied in her teeth. She gave him a bright smile. 'Just checking.'

'There's a bell in the galley. Ring it when the food's ready.'

For whom the bell tolls, Chellie thought glumly as she made her way down to the galley and looked around her. There was an electric oven, with a hob, and—oh, joy—a toaster and a cafetière waiting on the counter beside it. So far, so good, she thought, opening cupboards and drawers and finding crockery and cutlery. At least that bit would be easy-peasy.

She knew the theory of scrambled eggs, of course. Butter and milk, she told herself, and a lot of stirring. And, in her experience, someone else to do it.

She laid one of the tables in the saloon, then spooned

coffee into the pot, added boiling water, and carved some uneven slices off a loaf, slotting them with difficulty into the toaster.

She arranged the ham on plates, and began to beat up the eggs in a basin. The butter was beginning to turn brown in the pan as she added her mixture quickly and began to scrape at it with a fork, watching with dismay as it separated into long leathery strands.

At the same time a strong smell of scorching signalled that the bread was stuck in the toaster and needed to be poked out with a knife.

She felt like a wet rag as she finally rang the bell.

When Ash and Laurent arrived, she saw their brows lift as they inspected the plates she set in front of them. The ham, fortunately, was excellent, but no one lingered over their meal.

'This coffee's so weak I'm surprised it could crawl out of the pot,' Ash told her crushingly. 'You've cremated the toast. And as for this…' He stabbed at the rubbery mixture on his plate. 'I could use it to mend the tyres on a four-wheel drive. You said you could cook.'

'Or did you just make assumptions because of my gender?' Chellie shot back, furious at this condemnation of her efforts.

'Don't start that,' he advised brusquely. 'Preparing food is your job as part of the crew. The sole justification for your existence on this boat, as it happens, and gender doesn't feature in the equation. So make sure dinner is better.'

My God, did I really ever find him even remotely attractive? Chellie asked herself incredulously as he stalked out of the saloon and back up to the pilot house. It must have been temporary insanity brought on by stress.

Laurent accorded her a sympathetic smile. 'I bought some fresh beef in Santo Martino,' he told her. 'You can make a stew with it, *hein*?'

'No,' Chellie said in a hollow voice. 'I don't think I can, actually.'

Laurent sighed. 'I think maybe I should help, *cherie*, before Ash makes you walk the plank.'

Chellie stared at him. 'But he said you couldn't cook either.'

He shrugged. 'Maybe that was to arouse your sympathy, *cherie*, and make sure you sailed with us.' His eyes danced. 'After all, you are a very beautiful girl, and better to look at than the horizon all the time.'

She bit her lip, putting a self-conscious hand up to her hair. 'I'm a scarecrow.'

He patted her on the shoulder. 'It will grow,' he said gently.

He was brisk and competent as he supervised her cutting the meat into cubes and browning it in oil with garlic and onions. She cooked chopped vegetables in the oil too, then placed the whole concoction with red wine and vegetables, herbs and seasoning in a large electric crockpot which he produced from a cupboard.

'*C'est tout.*' Laurent switched on the pot and adjusted the setting. 'Now it cooks slowly until we are ready for it this evening.' He grinned at her. 'And you have learned how to feed a hungry man.'

Most of the hungry men I know feed themselves, Chellie returned silently. Using their platinum cards.

'Any more little jobs our gallant captain would like me to do?' she asked with spurious sweetness. 'Like swabbing the decks with my toothbrush?'

Laurent's smile faded, and he gave her an old-fashioned look. 'You might be wiser not to suggest it, *mademoiselle*.' He paused. 'You would prefer, perhaps, to have remained in Santo Martino?'

There was a silence, and Chellie swallowed. She said in a low voice,

'Did he tell you—where he found me—and why?'

'Yes, he told me.' Laurent nodded. 'It was a very bad time for you.'

'And it also makes me an ungrateful bitch,' she said bitterly.

He shrugged. 'Ash is no saint, *mademoiselle*. But which of us is?'

'I should have told him I couldn't cook.' Chellie sighed. 'But it would have made me sound so stupid—so useless.' She shook her head. 'I thought— Everyone cooks, so how hard can it be?'

He gave her a consoling pat on the shoulder. 'Well, you have discovered the answer to that, *ma petite*. But there are not many meals before St Hilaire,' he added encouragingly. 'Your present ordeal will soon be over.'

Maybe, Chellie thought when she was alone. But that doesn't mean I'm going to be able to forget in a hurry. And putting Ash Brennan out of my mind could be one of the hardest things I've ever done.

She felt the sudden pressure of tears, hot and heavy in her throat.

What's happening to me? she asked herself passionately. And how can I please make it stop? Because I don't want this. I don't need it. And, what's more to the point, neither does he.

It was useless telling herself that she was being a pathetic fool. That in reality she knew next to nothing about him. And that after they reached St Hilaire in all probability she would never set eyes on him again.

It's all true, she thought sadly. And it makes no difference—no difference at all. It's too late for that.

And she felt the knowledge—the sheer hurt of that bleak realisation—harden inside her like a stone.

She worked steadily, with just a suspicion of gritted teeth, clearing the washing up and tidying the galley, determined that Ash should have nothing else to criticise. But once that was finished she found herself at something of a loss.

Her position on board was frankly equivocal, she thought, grimacing. Stuck somewhere between non-paying passenger and failed cook. And popular on neither front.

She wondered if she should spend the day in her stateroom, out of sight and out of mind, with the handful of paperback books and magazines which she'd found in a cupboard in the saloon.

Except that was the coward's way out. And she didn't want Ash to gain the impression that she was deliberately avoiding him, in case he asked himself why.

So she would go and spend some time on the sundeck—and if he wanted to clap her in irons, good luck to him.

In her stateroom, she picked the least revealing of the bikinis on offer—plain black with a pretty voile overshirt patterned in black and white—but she still felt thoroughly self-conscious and a little daunted as she emerged into the brilliance of the sunshine.

As if I'm coming out of hibernation after a long winter, she thought wryly as she climbed to the sundeck. Or out of jail after a reprieve.

At the club, she'd almost become a creature of the night, spending most of the day asleep in an exhausted attempt to forget her fetid surroundings. Only aware of the weather outside when rain heavy as pebbles began drumming on the roof, or tropical lightning lit up the room like a laser show.

I'll never take fresh air and sunshine for granted again, she swore fervently.

Ash was there before her, sitting at the table, going through a sheaf of paperwork. He acknowledged her presence with a brief nod, but she felt he was simply preoccupied rather than unwelcoming.

Well, it was a start, she thought. She slipped off her shirt and stretched out on one of the cushioned loungers, closing her eyes, feeling the heat penetrating down to her bones, dispelling the last, lingering chill of fear.

She realised now that being afraid had become a way of life. That she'd begun waiting from hour to hour for the

next blow to fall. And that was insidious, because it withered hope and sapped the will to resist.

If Ash hadn't come, she thought, how long before she'd
have stopped caring what happened to her? Before she'd
yielded listlessly to whatever plans Mama Rita had for her?

In many ways it had been the same with her father, she
realised. What had been the point of fighting him when she
always lost? Maybe this was why Ramon had found her
such an easy victim. Because rebelling against her father in
such a basic way was her only chance of victory in their
war of attrition.

'Here.' Ash's voice broke curtly into her reverie, and she
looked up with a start to see him holding out a large tube
of cream to her.

'I'm sorry,' she said. 'I—I was miles away.'

'You'll be miles away in hospital if you're not careful.'
He uncapped the tube. 'Sunblock,' he said. 'Use plenty.'

'Oh,' Chellie said. 'Well—thank you.'

'Think nothing of it,' he returned politely. 'I didn't want
you to suffer the same fate as the toast, that's all.' And he
went back to the table and his papers.

Beast, thought Chellie, sending a muted glare to join him.
But maybe it was better this way. Because if he ever started
being nice to her then she would really be in trouble.

She applied the sunblock with conscientious care, then
settled back and opened one of the magazines she'd brought
with her and began glancing in a desultory way through its
glossy pages.

On the face of it, everything back to normal, she thought.
Only she knew, deep in her heart, that nothing would ever
be the same again.

She was disturbingly aware of him, seated only a few
yards away. She found she was registering every slight
movement, even the rustle of the papers as he turned them
over.

Before long I'll be counting the hours again, she thought
bitterly. Panicking about the length of the trip to St Hilaire.

Ash shuffled the papers together and rose. He said, 'I'm going to get Laurent a beer. Do you want anything?'

'A Coke, maybe.' Chellie reached for her shirt. 'Shall I get them?'

'Relax,' he advised lazily. 'You're like a cat on hot bricks.' He gave her a long look. 'What's the matter? Scared that Manuel is going to come over the horizon, flying the skull and crossbones and singing "Yo-ho-ho and a bottle of rum"?' He shook his head. 'Unlikely.'

She smiled tautly. 'But not impossible.'

'Roughly on the same level as being abducted by aliens.' He paused. 'Rats like Manuel don't stray far from their sewers.'

She said in a low voice, 'There was a time, not so long ago, when I wouldn't have believed that people like him— like Mama Rita—even existed. I know better now. And I never believed in miracles either,' she added. 'I'm having to rethink my position on them too, thanks to you.'

She hesitated. 'And I haven't thanked you, have I? Not really. Not as I should have done.' She bit her lip. 'Maybe now would be an appropriate time.'

'Did you sleep well last night?' Ash's tone was quizzical, and when she nodded he smiled at her swiftly, with a charm that made her heart lurch. 'Then that's all the thanks I need,' he said, and went.

Chellie subsided limply against her cushions. She'd felt that smile like the brush of his fingers across her skin.

She thought, Oh, God, I'll have to be careful. So very careful.

She could hear him talking to Laurent. Heard the sound of their laughter. Men comfortable in their skins, at ease together.

I wish I could be like that with him, she thought. Relaxed. No edge.

Able to meet and part as friends.

But we're barely acquaintances. He walked into my life, and saved it, and soon he'll walk away again. In a few months, or even weeks, I'll be a vague memory. A half-forgotten incident. And to pretend anything else would be ludicrous.

Ash came back a few minutes later and put a bottle of Coke with a straw down beside her. He moved over to the rail and stood watching the boat's wake, apparently lost in thought as he drank his beer.

Chellie took a long swallow of her ice-cold drink to ease her dry throat, then she rose and went to stand beside him.

She said constrictedly, 'I—I'm really sorry about breakfast.' She took a deep breath. 'I—lied because I was afraid you'd leave me behind if I said I couldn't cook.'

'No,' he said, after a pause, 'I wouldn't have done that.' His mouth twisted. 'But I might have asked you to display one of your other talents instead.'

Chellie tensed, giving him a wary sideways glance. 'What do you mean?' She hoped he hadn't detected the faint tremor in her tone.

He said quietly, 'You have the most beautiful singing voice. I might have asked for an after-dinner serenade.'

She flushed, surprised. 'Thank you.'

'Did you sing professionally back in Britain?' The question sounded casual, but the blue eyes were curious.

Chellie shook her head. 'No. I was never able to have proper training.'

'Was that what you wanted?'

'Yes, at one time I wanted it very much.'

For a brief, painful moment she could remember how she'd begged to be allowed to enter for a scholarship to a leading academy, and how she'd been brusquely refused. What was more, her father had given instructions at her school that her musical studies were to cease with immediate effect. How many times had she cried herself to sleep in the weeks that followed? She'd lost count.

She said flatly, 'It just wasn't considered a viable career. And they were probably right.' She forced a determined smile. 'After all, I hardly wowed them at Mama Rita's.'

'Choose another audience,' he said. 'And, training or not, it might be a different story.' He slanted a faint grin at her. 'Besides, you made a profound impression on me. Or had you forgotten?'

Her flush deepened. 'No. But you aren't exactly the typical Mama Rita customer.' She paused. 'Whatever made you pick that particular bar?'

He shrugged. 'It sold alcohol.'

'Yes, but so did a dozen others. And that wasn't its main commodity, as you must have realised.'

'Yes, I knew.' He gave her a mocking glance. 'Never underestimate the depravity of the male sex, songbird.'

Chellie looked away. She said quietly, 'You don't look like someone who needs to pay for cheap thrills.'

'The thrills were certainly questionable.' Ash's voice was dry. 'Cheap they were not.'

She winced. 'I'd forgotten that.' She lifted her chin. 'And I've caused you enough problems already, so I don't intend you to be out of pocket as well. I—I will repay you some-how—some day.'

'Oh, forget it,' he said with a touch of impatience. 'God knows, I could do with a few credits on my moral balance sheet.'

There seemed to be no answer to that. Chellie was silent for a moment while she searched for a neutral subject. Eventually she said, 'This is a fabulous boat.'

'Thank you. I'll tell the owner you said so.'

'You said you were delivering it for him?' Her brow creased. 'From Santo Martino?'

'No, from La Tortuga. He'd just put in there when he was suddenly called away on business. So he needed someone to sail '*La Belle Rêve*' back to St Hilaire.'

'Is that where he lives?'

'Some of the time. But he's not there at the moment.'

'Oh,' she said. 'So, what were you doing in Santo Martino?'

'Fuel,' he said. 'Supplies. It's a good marina.'

'You must be great friends with this man,' she said. 'If he's prepared to trust you with his boat.'

'Ah,' he said lightly, 'but I'm eminently trustworthy.'

And his daughter, she thought. *Does he trust you with her too?* Thought it, but did not dare ask it aloud. Because it was too personal—and too revealing a question. Besides, it was none of her business.

He'd done her the greatest favour of her life, but that didn't compel him to reveal every detail of his private affairs to her.

Not that he ever would, she thought slowly. There was something about Ash Brennan—something closed and separate. You could probably know him for a dozen years and never do more than scratch the outer shell.

He seemed—totally self-sufficient. Complete in himself. So, even if he met a woman he wanted, would he be prepared to allow her into his heart and mind? Make the necessary emotional commitment? It seemed less than likely.

Maybe it's as well we're going different ways, she thought, *before I wreck my heart on his indifference.*

She hurried into speech again. 'Will you stay on St Hilaire for long?'

He shrugged. 'Possibly. My plans are flexible.'

'Is this what you do for a living? Skipper other people's boats?'

'I can turn my hand to all kinds of things,' he said. 'And you ask a lot of questions, songbird.'

She flushed again. 'I'm sorry. I'm just envious, I suppose, of all the freedom you seem to have.'

'No one is ever completely free,' he said. 'But I'm working on it.' He paused. 'And what about you, Michelle Greer? What are your plans for the next fifty years?'

She stared down at the sea. 'I'm not making any immediate plans,' she said in a low voice. 'I don't seem to be very good at it.'

'I'd quite like to ask a few questions of my own.' He drank some of his beer. 'Are you up for it?'

'Why not?' Chellie returned with a touch of defensiveness.

'Oh, I can think of several reasons.' Leaning on the rail, he sent her a fleeting grin. 'You're a bit of a mystery, Michelle.'

'Really?' She raised her eyebrows. 'You, of course, are an open book.'

'I do hope not,' he said softly. 'How dull it would be if everyone I met could guess how things would end.'

'You don't have to worry about that,' she said. 'Ask away. I have nothing to hide,' she added, mentally crossing her fingers.

'Is that a fact?' His drawl was amused. 'Then that probably makes you unique. But we won't pursue that—or not at the moment, anyway.' He paused. 'How did you come to be in South America?'

'I went there to be married.'

If she'd expected a reaction she was disappointed. He simply nodded thoughtfully.

'So,' he said. 'What happened to the happy bridegroom?'

'He—changed his mind. Perhaps, like you, he preferred his freedom.'

'Why come all this way for a wedding?'

Chellie shrugged defensively. 'Lots of people get married in exotic locations. As it happens, Caribbean islands are immensely popular.'

He nodded. 'Santo Martino less so, I'd have thought.'

'The actual ceremony was going to be held on Ramon's estate up country. He said the easiest way to reach it was by river, so we came here to catch a boat.

She attempted a laugh, trying to make a joke of it. 'Instead, I caught a virus.'

'So you said. And Ramon?'

'Perhaps he took the boat home. He didn't wait around to tell me.'

'And of course the boat wasn't the only thing he took.' He sounded almost matter-of-fact.

Her mouth tightened. 'No. Do we really have to go through all this? It's hardly one of my favourite memories.'

'Are you still in love with him?'

'*What?*' She stared at him.

'It's a simple enough question. If he suddenly appeared here on deck now—would you forgive him—take him back?'

'Certainly,' she said. 'When all hell freezes over.'

'Yet once you cared enough to come halfway across the world with him.'

'I thought I did,' Chellie said tightly. 'I also believed that he cared for me. I was wrong on both counts.'

'So,' he said, 'when did you realise you weren't in love?'

She thought, *When we were in bed together. When I felt his hands on me—and he pushed himself into me. When he was hurting me, and he wouldn't stop...*

She said, keeping her tone deliberately light, 'I think I've told you quite enough. All other information is on a "need to know" basis.'

He moved swiftly, sharply. Came to her, taking her face between his hands and looking deeply into her startled green eyes.

He said softly, 'And just how the hell, songbird, would you know *what* I need?'

He let her go just as suddenly and walked away, leaving her leaning against the rail as if it was her sole support in the whole world. And staring after him with one shaking hand pressed to her parted lips.

CHAPTER FIVE

SHE almost called to him. Almost asked him to come back. She wanted him to explain what he'd said—and the note of suppressed anger that she'd detected beneath the words.

But some providence—or maybe it was simple self-preservation—kept her silent. Because it was not just words that she wanted from him, and she knew it. Nor was it anger. No, although she was ashamed to admit it, her needs were very different.

She went numbly back to her lounger and lay down, struggling to regain her composure. Her face still burned where he had touched her. His touch had been light, but she felt as if she would bear the marks of his fingers through all eternity.

'Oh, God,' she whispered to herself, 'why did he have to do that? Why did he have to put his hands on me?'

And that was not the worst of it. He'd been so near to her that she'd found herself breathing the erotic male scent of his skin. She'd been aware that her nipples were hardening urgently against the flimsy cups of the bikini, felt the first scalding rush of arousal between her thighs.

The desperation of her own need had scared her. Had almost overwhelmed her.

If he had taken her in his arms she would have yielded completely. And he must have known that. He could not have been oblivious to the sheer physicality of her response. To that shock of trembling desire.

He had been as aware of her as she'd been of him— hadn't he?

But—he hadn't followed through. Instead he'd walked away. And perhaps, she thought painfully, his words could be interpreted as a warning to her not to expect more than he was prepared to give. He'd rescued her, given her temporary sanctuary, but that was as far as it went.

He'd probably decided she was more trouble than she was worth, and wanted no further involvement. And once they reached St Hilaire all contact between them would be severed.

She supposed she should be grateful to him for not taking advantage of her vulnerability, but she couldn't feel thankful. Or not yet, at least.

She closed her eyes, forbidding herself to cry, ashamed of her own reactions—her own weakness. Her experiences in Santo Martino must have affected her more deeply than she'd realised. That was the only explanation.

I don't seem to be the same person any more, she told herself. I don't think or feel as I did. I don't know myself. It's ludicrous—and it can't be allowed to go on. I've got to build up my immune system again—particularly against men like Ash Brennan.

She would certainly need to pull herself together before they arrived at St Hilaire. She couldn't afford to give the impression that she was still dependent on Ash in any way—that she was in want of his continued help. She had to show by her attitude that she'd recovered and was ready to take charge of her life.

And she would manage alone, she added grimly. She would have to, because she had no intention of asking her father for assistance.

Not when she'd put herself in terrible danger and come within a whisker of wrecking her entire life in order to escape his control in the first place.

Because that was what had happened. She could see that so clearly now. See that Ramon had simply seemed a lifeline—a way of resolving her frustration and unhappiness with her existence. Drastic but effective.

I wished myself into love with him, she thought, her mouth twisting wryly. He seemed to be offering me a lifestyle that was the opposite to everything I'd ever known. Something that had a surface glamour all its own.

But getting away from my father was always the main attraction, even if I didn't realise it at the time.

I had to learn it the hard way, she thought, shivering.

But there was no substance to my relationship with Ramon, and even if he'd turned out to be a thoroughly decent guy it couldn't have lasted.

Looking back, she realised she'd had doubts even before they'd left England. There had been details about his background that didn't jell. Vague contradictions in the stories he'd told her that should have alerted her.

If I'd given myself time to stop and think, she told herself with sudden energy, I wouldn't have gone to the end of the street with him. And I'd have saved myself a hell of a lot of misery—and sheer terror.

Above all, I would not have met Ash, and that, in itself, would have been a kind of safety. A security I've lost for ever now. Because he's under my skin—in my blood.

And the first thing I need to do on St Hilaire is get away from him, as far and as fast as I can. And start to forget. Or try to, at least.

She found herself shivering.

Ash strode into the pilot house, his body taut, his mouth set.

Laurent swung round in his leather chair, giving him a quizzical look. *'Ça va?'*

'Not particularly.' Ash flung himself into the adjoining seat, his expression brooding.

'Then I regret I must add to your troubles. Another fax from Victor. There has been a change of plan.' He paused. 'The girl is now to be taken directly to England, and handed over there.'

'Not by me,' Ash returned curtly. 'The deal was St Hilaire—nowhere else—and that's how it's going to stand.' He shook his head. 'Oh, God, I knew I should never have got involved in this.'

Laurent grinned wickedly. 'But you were ideal—the only choice, *mon vieux*. Your irresistible charm was essential to entice *la petite* Michelle away from her lover. How were we to know that the *affaire* had already ended in tears?'

A muscle moved beside Ash's mouth. 'He told her he had a country estate.' He gave a short laugh. 'A shanty in a clearing, I don't doubt.'

Laurent gave a philosophical shrug. 'Then it is as well, perhaps, that it ended while she still had some of her illusions.'

Ash sighed harshly. 'I don't think she had many to start with. And she'll be left with even fewer when she realises she's just swapped one cage for another. That she's been bought and sold. What price her illusions then?'

'You are in danger of breaking your own rules, my friend,' Laurent warned quietly. 'Do the job—earn the money—don't get involved. Isn't that you've always said? How you have survived?'

'I haven't forgotten,' Ash said shortly. 'And the rules still apply.' He sighed again. 'And now I'd better fax Victor and tell him to give Clive Greer a message—that I'll keep his daughter under wraps on St Hilaire until he hands over the money and comes to fetch her. In person. As agreed.'

'He will not like that.'

Ash shrugged. 'Victor and I stopped agreeing about a lot of things some time ago. That's one of the reasons I decided to make this my last assignment and move on.'

'I know that, *mon ami*. But I did not, in fact, refer to Victor. I meant Clive Greer—a very different opponent, I think. Maybe you should be careful.'

'I intend to be.' Ash sent him a swift bleak smile.

And thought, as he bent forward on the pretext of studying the instruments, I have to be—for all kinds of reasons…

Chellie had every intention of thinking positively, but it wasn't easy when her unhappy thoughts insisted on marching round and round in her head as if they were on a treadmill.

Instead of asking Ash a lot of questions he didn't wish to answer, she'd have done better to find out more about St Hilaire, she thought ruefully, applying more sunblock to her exposed skin. And that way she might have avoided undergoing an interrogation herself—and its aftermath.

But the plan she'd formulated in Santo Martino, to find the local consular office and ask for assistance, still seemed good to her, although she would certainly need to conceal her father's identity if she wanted them to help her in any practical sense.

Because they would feel Sir Clive was the obvious person for her to approach, particularly if a financial loan was involved, and she was certainly going to need money to get herself out of the Caribbean.

But she would not ask her father for assistance under any circumstances. For one thing it would put her under a crushing psychological disadvantage to present herself to him as a loser, although she didn't doubt that was how he thought of her anyway.

But I don't need my nose rubbed in it, she told herself.

And now that she'd managed to win herself a 'Get Out of Jail Free' card, she was determined not to relinquish it, however hard the going might become. And no job, no home and no prospects was about as hard as it could get.

By the time she faced her father again she had to hold some kind of winning hand.

Somehow I have to be in a position to dictate my own terms, she thought with resolution.

What she did need, however, in the short term, was her passport. She'd assumed that once they were safely out of Santo Martino Ash would simply hand it over, yet it hadn't been mentioned since she came on board, and this made her uneasy.

It might just have slipped his mind, of course, but somehow she did not think so. There didn't seem to be much the matter with his mental processes.

In fact, she had the distinct impression that he was invariably several steps ahead of her, and maybe it was time she redressed the balance a little.

After all, she argued, her passport was a valuable piece of her personal property. Certainly the local consul would want to see it as proof of her identity, so she had every right to retrieve it without further reference to anyone.

And how hard could that be? *La Belle Rêve* was pretty sumptuous, but it was just a boat with all the limitations that implied. And there could only be so many hiding places.

The obvious place to look, of course, was in Ash's sleeping quarters, she realised, chewing her lip. And there couldn't be too many cabins to search before she found the right one.

She left her magazine open beside the sun cream on her lounger, to indicate to all interested parties that her absence was only temporary, and, slipping her shirt over her bikini, went below, sauntering casually while she was in the view of the pilot house, then moving in swift and silent caution on bare feet once she was out of sight.

Now, she told herself, it was just a question of opening doors. She discovered the crew quarters first, but only one of the bunks was being used there and that, to judge from the clothing and personal items scattered around, belonged to Laurent.

Next she tried the stateroom next to her own, her pulses flickering oddly at the idea that Ash might be sleeping just on the other side of a thin wooden partition, but the neat twin berths were clearly unoccupied.

Which meant that he must be using the master suite in the stern.

Establishing himself as the man in charge in every possible way, Chellie thought caustically. I should have realised—and gone there first.

She opened the door and looked in. It had been furnished to impress, there was little doubt of that. The wide bed, piled with pillows, occupied the centre of the room like an ivory satin island, and the fitted wardrobes and dressing chests had been made from some expensive pale wood. Her feet sank into the thick carpet as she made her way across the stateroom.

The khaki pants he'd been wearing yesterday were lying across the laundry bin in the luxurious shower room, but a swift search soon revealed that their pockets had been emptied.

She swore softly, and turned her attention to the night tables that flanked the bed, but all she found were a few coins, a clean handkerchief, and a paperback copy of the new John Grisham.

And one other item that stopped her in her tracks: a framed photograph of a girl—blonde, slim and pretty in vest top and shorts—smiling with total confidence into the camera.

Chellie picked it up and studied it, aware that her heartbeat had altered. That it was now thrumming slowly and painfully against her ribcage.

The owner's daughter? she wondered. Or someone completely different? The current top of a long and varied list?

And right there beside the bed, where it would undoubtedly be the last thing he saw at night and the first in the morning.

She replaced it, swallowing past the sudden ache in her throat.

Well, what had she expected? she asked in self-derision. He was A list attractive and seriously footloose. Not at all the type to lead a celibate life. She'd known that from the first moment.

Maybe she was just surprised that he cared enough to keep such a personal memento. He must really consider himself spoken for, she thought. Which explained a good deal.

Suddenly she didn't want to continue the search any longer. She needed quite seriously to get out of the room and close the door firmly behind her—in more ways than one, she thought, biting her lip.

She had to think, and for that she needed solitude—and privacy.

She'd just reached her own stateroom, had her fingers on the doorhandle, when Ash said, 'So here you are.'

She swung round, gasping. She'd been so lost in thought that she'd been quite oblivious to his approach.

She thought, *A moment earlier and he'd have caught me. I need to keep my wits about me.*

She managed to keep her voice reasonably level. 'You—startled me.'

'Evidently.' His tone was sardonic. 'I must learn to cough discreetly.' He studied her, frowning a little. 'What are you doing?'

'Looking for a little peace,' she returned, lifting her chin in challenge. 'I wasn't aware I required your permission.'

His mouth tightened. 'You don't. I was simply—concerned. I thought maybe you'd had too much sun.' He studied her. 'You look—flushed.'

Perhaps I do, she thought, but that has nothing to do with the heat of the day.

She shrugged. 'I'm not aware of it,' she said, deliberately casual, trying to ignore the fact that they were facing each other in a confined space. 'Was there anything else?'

'Actually, some lunch would be good.' He paused. 'Nothing too onerous. Just some soup and a few sandwiches, perhaps.'

'Fine,' she said. 'I'll ring when it's ready.'

He gave her another searching look. 'Are you really all right?' he asked abruptly.

'Never better.' She flashed him a meaningless smile. 'Now, if you'll excuse me, I'll get back to my duties.'

Ash propped a shoulder against the wall, effectively

blocking her retreat. 'I'm beginning to realise how those old Roman slavedrivers must have felt,' he remarked.

'Well, don't worry about it,' Chellie said crisply. 'I'm sure any stirrings of compunction will soon wear off. At least by the time we get to St Hilaire, anyway.' She paused. 'When will that be, exactly?'

'Exactitude isn't a particular virtue in the Caribbean,' he said. 'But we're aiming for tomorrow afternoon.' His mouth twisted wryly. 'So my opportunities to crack the whip are therefore numbered.'

'My,' she said. 'Things are getting better all the time.'

He said courteously, 'I'm glad you think so.' He studied her for a moment, brows lifted. 'Do I take it you're not enjoying the voyage?'

'Was enjoyment the intention?' Her laugh was brief and deliberately artificial. 'I hadn't realised.'

He said slowly, 'It's also escaped your notice, apparently, that I've been fighting quite hard not to make a bad situation worse.'

'How could you possibly manage that?' She sent him a mutinous glance.

He said quietly, 'Like this.' And pulled her forward into his arms. His hands slid round her body under the loose shirt, pinning her against him, making her wholly aware that they were both almost naked. Forcing her to recognise that he was unashamedly aroused.

She had raised her hands instinctively to push him away. Instead her palms encountered the naked muscularity of his chest and lingered there of their own volition, savouring the smooth heat of his skin and the harsh thud of his heartbeat.

Ash bent his head, the blue eyes glinting down at her like sun-drenched azure, and Chellie's lips parted in a gasp of shock. She tried to say something—to find words of pro-test—of denial, even—but then his mouth closed on hers, warm and totally possessive, and the chance was lost—if it had ever truly existed.

His lips were moving on hers, softly but with purpose,

sending messages of deliberate sensual demand to her reeling brain. He was teasing her tongue with his, coaxing her to respond. To grant him the total access to her surprised mouth that he was seeking.

Her head fell back and her lashes drifted down, preparing her for this initial surrender. Presaging what might follow.

She found she was lifting her arms and winding them round his neck, pressing even closer to him, so that her breasts in their fragile covering grazed the wall of his chest.

His kiss deepened instantly, passionately, and she tasted hunger on his mouth. Recognised it because she shared it. And because she needed so desperately for it to be assuaged.

Ash pushed the shirt from her shoulders, letting it drop to the floor. His hands were stroking her skin, tracing the vulnerable line of her backbone, brushing the sensitive nerve-endings, making her sigh and quiver in mounting excitement.

She felt him unsnap the clip that held her bikini top and slide down the straps. The flimsy cups fell away, releasing her bare breasts to the caress of his fingers.

His touch was gentle, but very sure, circling her hardening nipples, encouraging them to some peak of sweet intensity she had never known before or even dreamed was possible. Making her glory in this new intimacy.

Her legs were shaking under her and she leaned back, seeking the support of the stateroom door.

The note of her breathing had changed, and her pulses were going crazy. She could feel the fiery strength of his erection against her thighs, and knew that neither of them could wait much longer.

All she had to do was open the door behind her, she realised with a swift intake of breath—and the bed would be there waiting for them.

And this time, her frantic body told her, consummation would be very different.

This time.

Suddenly, unwillingly, she was back in that first hotel

room, spreadeagled across the awful bed and its creaking mattress, with Ramon on top of her, his face contorted as he drove for his own satisfaction. Ramon—hurting her and not caring. Ramon—using her without love.

Just as Ash would do—if she allowed it.

She heard herself make a small hoarse sound of negation. Found that she was pushing at Ash with new-found strength, struggling to free herself, the image of the photograph on his night table forcing its way into her reluctant memory. Reminding her that they were still virtual strangers and that he had a life about which she knew nothing.

At the same time, to him she was nothing more than a body he had briefly coveted in Mama Rita's club, but not enjoyed. Or not then, at least.

She could see now that he'd simply been—biding his time. Waiting for the moment when she would simply fall into his hand.

Well, she owed him, and she knew it, but she could not repay the debt with sex. He would take her with more finesse than Ramon, she had no doubt of that, but his purpose would be the same—to satisfy a transient desire. And she would not allow herself to be used like that again, only to be discarded when he chose to walk away.

Ramon had ignored her reluctance, and her protests. He'd imposed himself on her with almost casual brutality.

Ash, however, released her at once, staring down at her, his brows snapping together. 'What's the matter?'

She stared down at the boards under her feet. 'I—I can't.' Her voice trembled. 'I—I just remembered something. Someone.'

Her words seemed to fall into a long and terrible silence. When at last she ventured to look up at him, she saw his face cold as a stone mask.

'Ash,' she said. And again, 'Ash—I'm sorry.'

She wanted to explain to him, but thoughts were churning in her head and she couldn't form a coherent sentence.

'No,' he said. 'Don't be sorry.' The words were curt and

clipped. His smile glittered without warmth. 'I also have things I need to remember.'

He paused. 'I suppose I should thank you for reminding me. But I don't feel particularly grateful right now. So let's agree we've both been saved from a really bad mistake and leave it there.' He gave a slight shrug. 'After all, nothing really happened.'

From some far distance she heard herself say huskily, 'Didn't it?'

'It was a kiss, songbird.' His voice was quiet, but it bit. 'And you've been kissed before, and far more than that, so don't treat me to any virginal vapours. Just forget it ever took place. As I shall.'

He stood aside, pushing sweat-dampened hair back from his forehead. 'And now, please don't let me keep you from your real duties any longer.'

She had to reach down to retrieve her shirt and bikini top. When she straightened, her face was burning. She hoped without much conviction that he would think it was down to the exertion of bending, rather than the confusion of embarrassment and frustration that was consuming her entire body.

She put on the shirt, dragging its edges together to conceal her exposed skin as she eased her way past him.

Once clear, she risked a swift glance over her shoulder to see if he was still there—if he was watching her go with any kind of regret. But he'd disappeared, presumably to his cabin, and she realised she could make her escape in relative peace.

She went quickly up the companionway, only to find when she reached the galley that she was panting as if she'd just taken part in a marathon.

Her first action was to fumble her way back into her bikini top and fasten the shirt over it. She was only sorry the buttons didn't reach to her throat.

The rasp of the cloth against her awakened flesh was a torment she could do without.

She ran cold water from the tap over the tumultuous pulses in her wrists, and splashed cool droplets on to her face in an attempt to calm her hectic flush.

He'd said forget it, she thought with a kind of desperation, but how could she? Especially when all she wanted was to hide away somewhere in a dark corner where she would never have to set eyes on him again.

But there was small chance of that in the confines of *La Belle Rêve*. And in practical terms she was going to have to face him pretty soon, anyway, because she had lunch to prepare and serve.

Oh, God, she groaned inwardly, scanning the cupboards for tinned soup. How much worse can it all get?

It made her squirm to remember how easily she'd melted into his embrace, as if it had been invented for her alone, when what she should really have done was fight him off at once.

In fact, she should never have allowed the situation to develop in the first place, she thought gloomily. She should have remembered why she was there and kept her dealings with him on a strictly businesslike basis.

Even when he mentioned St Hilaire you never asked him for your passport, although it was the perfect opportunity, she castigated herself bitterly. Even if you'd made him mad, at least it would have kept him at arm's length.

She heard footsteps crossing the saloon and tensed. Had Ash noticed that she'd been in his cabin? she thought frantically. Had she moved something, or left a drawer open? And what excuse could she offer if he accused her of prying?

Except I don't need an excuse, she told herself swiftly. He has my property. I want it back. End of story.

But when she turned, prepared to give battle, she saw with relief that it was Laurent.

'May I offer any help?'

'I think I can manage.' She grimaced. 'Even I ought to be able to open a can of soup.'

'Are you sure? You seem a little flushed—out of sorts.'

She shrugged a shoulder. 'Too much sun,' she said lightly. 'I'm still not used to it.'

'Ah,' he said, his eyes considering her shrewdly. 'That might account for it.' He paused. 'I took some savoury pastries from the freezer earlier. Would you like me to heat them?'

'Yes, please,' Chellie said gratefully.

She poured the creamy vegetable soup into a pan, and began to warm it gently while Laurent busied himself at the oven.

She said, 'I just hope we get to St Hilaire before I poison everyone.'

He clicked his tongue. 'That is not fair. You should not put yourself down in such a way, *mademoiselle*.'

'Please,' she said. 'My other friends call me Chellie.'

His brows lifted, 'You flatter me—Chellie. *Merci du compliment*.'

'So, tell me something about St Hilaire?' She kept her voice bright, interested. 'I gather it's not very big?'

'No,' he said. 'But my home is there, so I think it very beautiful.'

'Are you married?'

'Yes.' His face relaxed into a smile. 'And I have a son and a daughter.'

Chellie remembered there had been family photos in his cabin, but could not say so, of course. She said, 'They must miss you—when you're away like this.'

He shrugged. 'It does not happen so often.'

'Oh,' she said. 'Then this isn't how you earn your living—sailing other people's boats?'

'No,' he said. 'On St Hilaire I manage a banana plantation. And I have a boat of my own,' he added with a touch of dryness. 'I like to fish.'

Chellie hesitated, fighting with herself and losing. She said, trying to sound casual, 'And Ash—does he live on the island too?'

'There—and in other places.' He paused, giving a slight shrug. 'Unlike myself, he is a single man. So—he enjoys his freedom.'

'Yes,' she said. 'I'm sure he does.' *But for how much longer?* she asked herself, remembering the photograph beside his bed.

She concentrated her attention fiercely on the soup. After a moment or two, she said, 'Laurent—will you tell me something?'

'If I can.' He sounded faintly wary.

She drew a breath. 'Is Ash sorry that he rescued me? That he brought me out of that awful place?'

Laurent hesitated. 'I think, *cherie*, he regrets there was ever a necessity to do so.'

Her smile was wry. 'I'm sorry too.' She swirled a spoon in the soup, watching tiny bubbles begin to form. She said, 'But with Ash there's more to it than that—isn't there?'

He spread his hands. 'In life there are always—complications.'

She gave a wintry smile. 'And I'm one of those complications?'

He shook his head. 'I think I have already said too much.' He became businesslike. 'The pastries require five more minutes. There is salad in the refrigerator, also vinaigrette dressing in a small jar. Ash suggested that we eat on deck.'

'Fine,' she said, over-brightly. 'But I'll have my meal here. Less—complicated, you understand.'

Laurent gave her a quizzical look as he prepared to depart. 'I think that I begin to,' he murmured. 'Perhaps it may be better for you to—stay out of the sun, *cherie*.' And he went off, whistling under his breath.

Lunch was not as difficult as she'd feared, after all. Ash barely looked at her as he thanked her with cool politeness for the tray of food she set in front of them. Nor did he query her failure to join them.

Perhaps he was glad not to have to face her, Chellie thought as she ate her solitary meal.

Once it was all finished, and cleared away, Chellie went to her stateroom and took a long cool shower, changing back into the clothes she'd worn earlier.

No more chasing a tan, she told herself. In future it would be safer to cover up.

Now she needed something to occupy her—something that would stop her thinking again, because there was no guarantee that she could keep her thoughts under sufficient control for her own peace of mind.

She'd noticed there were cleaning materials in a locker near the crews' quarters, and she decided to turn her attention to the saloon.

If her father were here now, he wouldn't believe his eyes, she thought, applying polish to a table surface and rubbing vigorously, but for the first time in her life, she actually felt useful.

The scent of the casserole was beginning to permeate through from the galley, and she sniffed with real appreciation as she worked.

The events of the past twenty-four hours notwithstanding, she was beginning to see the attraction of life on board. Maybe she could seriously learn to cook and become part of the crew on another boat—preferably in a different ocean on the other side of the world.

Although she could well imagine her father's reaction to the news that she'd opted to become a sea-going skivvy. His cold displeasure.

She paused, wiping a few beads of perspiration from her forehead, aware of a faint shiver of uneasiness, as if she'd conjured up his actual presence.

Which was ridiculous, she told herself, resuming her vigorous rubbing, because Sir Clive was hundreds of miles away and the Caribbean was the last place he'd look for her. If, of course, he bothered to look at all, she conceded wryly.

Her elopement with Ramon would have made him very angry. So angry, probably, that he'd written off his unsatisfactory daughter with the same icy finality he'd show a bad debt. A line drawn and no further reference made.

My God, she thought. How many times have I seen him do it? So why should he treat me any differently?

Besides, Ramon had covered their tracks with extreme care. She could remember how impressed she'd been with his caution, the deliberate false trails that he'd laid. His insistence that they should not be followed. And how she'd naïvely interpreted it as his genuine wish to shield her from her father's wrath by putting themselves beyond his reach and winning their freedom.

Nice plan, she acknowledged ruefully. Yet its only achievement had been to enmesh her in a different kind of slavery.

And one that, in her heart, she had no real wish to escape.

It was an acknowledgement that struck her with all the force of a hammer-blow.

Chellie straightened slowly, feeling pain stir inside her with icy and corroding bitterness as she suddenly found herself reliving those all too short moments in Ash's arms. As she tasted once more the drugging sweetness of his kiss on her lips.

And stopped there, gasping, shaking her head in a despairing attempt to bring herself back to reality.

She said aloud, 'Don't do this to yourself, Michelle. Wake up and smell the coffee. Start repeating ten times a day, "There is no future with Ash Brennan" until you learn some sense at last.'

And tried to ignore the tiny warning voice in her brain which whispered that it might already be much too late. That she could be lost for ever.

CHAPTER SIX

ASH, of course, must never know how she felt.

That was what she kept repeating to herself, over and over again, as this seemingly endless day drew towards its close.

He must never be allowed to suspect, even for a moment, the riot of emotional confusion churning inside her.

I'd rather be back at Mama Rita's than have him guess how I'm feeling right now, she thought, wincing, as she went down to her stateroom to change for dinner.

She needed somehow to practise his own brand of cool indifference if she was to survive the remainder of this short voyage with her pride undamaged.

And when they reached St Hilaire she had to walk away without looking back. Grateful, but casual. Drawing a line under the whole affair.

No regrets, she thought, swallowing past a sudden tightness in her throat, and no recriminations—no matter how difficult that might be.

Because, although she might be able to keep her pride intact, she could not make any similar guarantees about her heart.

She groaned inwardly. Oh, God, she thought wretchedly, what am I doing to myself?

First Ramon—and now this—this disaster.

Did she never learn? she demanded of herself with savage intensity. Was she really planning to be a loser all her life, sighing for a whole series of Mr Wrongs?

And wasn't she making far too much of it all anyway? After all, as Ash had said himself, nothing had really happened. He'd made his play, been turned down, and shrugged it off.

Which indicated fairly bruisingly the relative unimportance of the encounter in his scheme of things, she thought unhappily. As far as he was concerned the point of no return had by no means been reached. Whereas as soon as his mouth had touched hers she'd gone up in flames—ready to give him anything he asked for.

And it was small consolation to tell herself that, in fact, she'd been the first one to draw back. Because it should never have been allowed to happen at all. And belated second thoughts didn't change a thing.

For God's sake, she castigated herself, I hardly know him. It may seem an eternity, but the truth is that he walked into my life less than forty-eight hours ago. And that is no basis for any kind of relationship—and certainly not a one-night stand. I'm worth more than that.

Besides, it went across every principle she had ever possessed. She'd believed that she was being seriously courted by Ramon, yet she'd held out against him for weeks on end, telling herself it would make their eventual union on their wedding night doubly precious.

She looked at herself in the mirror, running her fingers regretfully through the short, feathery spikes of black hair.

She seemed to have become a stranger to herself in all kinds of ways, she thought, sighing. But then for the last few weeks of her life survival had been the name of the game. She could afford nothing else.

And that was the situation she'd be forced to battle with for the foreseeable future.

Meanwhile, there was tonight to get through. And it was even more important not to lurk out of the way in the saloon or her own stateroom, as if she was too scared to face him. That would be instant self-betrayal.

She needed to be smiling and totally insouciant—as if she didn't have a care in the world and those few devastating moments in his arms had been shrugged aside as trivial. That was the way to play it—the only way.

She'd taken something quiet and unobtrusive from the

wardrobe, but now she thought, To hell with it, selecting instead with a certain defiance an ankle-length wraparound skirt, with crimson tropical flowers on a creamy background, topped by a square-necked, short-sleeved blouse in the same vibrant colour as the flowers.

Go out in style, she told herself, smoothing the silky fabric over her slim hips and crushing down the wayward thought that maybe Ash might also be left with something to regret.

Because the words 'if only' would feature rarely, if ever, in his vocabulary, and she knew it. And she'd be an even bigger fool if she hoped for anything else.

So—I'm a fool, she thought, and sighed soundlessly.

The casserole was delicious, served with a mound of fluffy rice and some tiny green beans which Laurent had shown her how to turn lightly in butter.

'Amazing,' Ash commented when he put down his fork. He gave her a brief smile across the table, which she'd set with small candles in pretty glass shades. 'You seem to have widened your repertoire since this morning.'

Chellie murmured something, then concentrated her attention on the remaining grains of rice on her own plate.

In spite of all her good resolutions, she was still finding Ash a disturbing dinner companion. He too had apparently decided to make an effort for their last night at sea, and was wearing well-cut dark pants with an open-necked white shirt that set off his tan. His blond hair was still darkened by damp from the shower, and she was tinglingly aware of the faint muskiness of some expensive cologne lingering on his skin.

He and Laurent had been involved in some low-voiced, forceful conversation when she'd first entered the wheelhouse, trying to hide her feeling of self-consciousness. He'd paused instantly, his brows lifting sharply, his attention completely arrested as he looked at her.

It had been only momentary. A breath later and he'd

turned back to Laurent. But for those few seconds Chellie knew that he'd been looking at her. Seeing no one but her. And she'd seen the sudden flare in his eyes.

Now, she drew a steadying breath and made herself meet his gaze again across the table.

'I can't claim the credit,' she denied stiltedly. 'I was coached by an expert.' She turned to the man beside her. 'Thank you, Laurent.'

He shrugged in self-deprecation. 'I had an apt pupil.' He paused. 'I have been saying to Ash that he should make you a permanent member of the crew.'

There was a silence, then from somewhere Chellie managed to produce a laugh that sounded genuinely amused.

'I don't think that would appeal to either of us,' she said cheerfully.

'Besides, I have a life to get on with.' She looked back at Ash. 'And *apropos* of that—may I have my passport back, please?'

'Right now?' He drank some of the red wine in his glass, leaning back in his chair. 'Why—are you planning to swim for it?'

'Not unless I have to.' *Be cool, be casual. Keep the joke going.* 'But I'm going to need it as soon as we get to the island, as proof of identity for the local consul.'

'Then there's no great hurry.' He was watching her from under lowered lids. 'Because tomorrow is Saturday and the office will be shut until Monday.'

'Shut?' Chellie could not conceal her dismay. 'Oh, no, not again, surely?' Being at Mama Rita's had made her lose all track of time, it seemed. 'But what if there's an emergency?'

Ash shrugged. 'We tend not to have them.' He paused. 'And I don't think your problems would be considered in that light anyway,' he added flatly.

She stiffened. 'You mean it's all right for me to be stranded as long as the consul gets his round of golf?'

'Set of tennis, I think,' he corrected blandly. 'And don't worry—you won't be sleeping on the beach.'

She lifted her chin. 'Says who?'

His mouth twisted mockingly. 'Well, the local police, for a start. They take a dim view of vagrancy.'

She bit her lip. 'Then would it be possible for me to remain on the boat—just until Monday morning?' She hated having to ask him for another favour—detested the faint note of entreaty she detected in her own voice.

Ash shook his head. 'I'm afraid the owner wouldn't permit that.'

Swallowing, Chellie made herself turn to Laurent. 'I don't suppose…?'

He spread his hands regretfully. 'My house is not large, *cherie*. And my wife, although the delight of my heart, is convinced all other women find me irresistible. I think your presence would make her—uneasy. You see the problem?'

'Yes,' she said, smiling resolutely. 'Of course. In that case I'd better head for the local Mama Rita's. I suppose there is one?'

'I doubt it.' Ash lit a cheroot. 'But isn't that a pretty drastic course to take, anyway?'

'Desperate situations,' she said, 'call for desperate measures.'

'Nevertheless,' he said slowly, 'there are a number of perfectly respectable places to stay on St Hilaire.'

'I'm sure there are,' she said. 'Places where they prefer their bills to be paid.'

'Naturally,' he said. 'So why don't you let me stake you to a room while you're on St Hilaire?'

Chellie's hands clenched together unseen in her lap. She said evenly, 'I don't think that's a very good idea.'

'No?' A slow smile curved his mouth. 'Would you care to elaborate?'

He was daring her to accuse him of wanting to share the room with her, she thought furiously. But she wasn't going to fall into that trap—particularly with Laurent as an interested audience.

Her mouth tightened, but she managed to keep her voice even. 'Because you've done quite enough to help already. It's time I started shouldering my own responsibilities.'

'Well, no-one would argue with that.' Ash shrugged a casual shoulder.

'But maybe you should wait until the odds aren't so heavily stacked against you.'

He made himself sound like the voice of sweet reason, Chellie realised, the gall and wormwood of thwarted rebellion stirring inside her. And as if butter wouldn't melt in his mouth...

'Come on, songbird.' His smile widened, suggesting that he'd accurately discerned her inner struggles and was amused by them. 'Let me lend a hand one last time. You can always pay me back.'

She swallowed. 'Please treat that as an absolute. Although I'm not sure when it will be possible,' candour forced her to add.

Ash tapped the ash from his cheroot.

'You could always pay me something on account tonight,' he suggested softly. 'After all, you know what I really want.'

Chellie found herself going rigid, then caught the wicked glint in his eyes and relaxed again.

She said lightly, 'Why not? After all, I didn't really cook the dinner, so I owe you already.' She paused. 'Any special requests?' she added, sending him a challenging look.

'Oh, Laurent's the musician round here.' Ash turned to him. 'Why don't you get your guitar, *mon vieux*? Michelle is going to sing to us.'

Laurent's brows lifted. '*Vraiment?* Then I should be honoured.'

Left alone with Ash, Chellie found tension seeping back as reason and desire fought a secret battle inside her.

She looked out at the moonlight streaming across the water. She said with a touch of uncertainty, 'It's—beautiful tonight.'

'Yes.' She realised that he was looking straight at her, not following the direction of her gaze at all. 'Very lovely.' His blue gaze rested meditatively on her parted lips, then moved downward to the swell of her breasts under the brief top and lingered, as if he was indulging a cherished memory.

In spite of herself, she felt her skin warm under his scrutiny. She could also remember, all too well, the arousing play of his fingers on her naked flesh, and how she'd longed to feel the caress of his lips against her heated nipples.

She thought achingly, Don't—don't do this to me—please...

She had to break the spell somehow. She began to reach for the used dishes. 'I—I ought to clear the table.'

'Laurent and I will do it,' he said, adding laconically, 'Save your strength for later.'

'Later?' She could have bitten her tongue. The query had been far too sharp—too pointed. It had sounded nervous. But then why shouldn't it—after the way he'd just been looking at her?

'For your singing,' he said. 'I understand it takes a lot of breath control?'

'Oh,' Chellie said, feeling foolish. 'Well—yes.'

He drew on the cheroot, watching her reflectively, his eyes shadowed by the sweep of his lashes—unreadable. 'That colour really suits you,' he said eventually. 'But I'm sure you know that already.'

'My first and last dinner on the boat,' she said, speaking a little too quickly. 'I thought I should dress up a little.' She hesitated. 'It's lucky that—these things—her clothes—fit me.'

He smiled faintly. 'Very lucky.'

There was another silence. Ash reached across and stubbed out the remains of the cheroot.

She said, 'I—I didn't know that you smoked.'

'Why should you?' he said. 'I do it very rarely—mainly when I'm under pressure. But I'm well aware it's a bad habit which I shall have to break quite soon.'

She bit her lip. 'And—do you feel—pressured now?'

'Of course,' he said. 'I have an expensive boat to take to St Hilaire.' He paused. 'Among other considerations.'

This time, Chellie thought, she was not taking the bait.

She was thankful to hear Laurent returning. As well as his guitar, he'd brought a tray with coffee and brandies.

'We should drink,' he announced, 'to our smooth passage so far, and our safe haven tomorrow.'

Smooth? Chellie thought bitterly, as she obediently echoed the toast. I feel as if I've been tossed from one storm to another. And it's not over yet. I still have to get away from St Hilaire, which is becoming less of a sanctuary by the minute.

'So.' Laurent sat back in his chair and applied some fine tuning to his guitar. 'What would you like to sing?'

Chellie shook her head. 'You play something,' she said. 'And if I know the words, I'll join in.'

He thought for a moment, then played a few soft chords, quite different from any of the lilting West Indian or Creole numbers she'd expected.

He said, 'You will know this, I think? "Plaisir d'Amour"?'

She knew it all right, with its echoing lament for betrayal and lost love, and for a moment she was tempted to ask him to choose another less potent melody. But that, she knew immediately, would be unwise. It would simply cause unnecessary fuss, might even turn an unwanted spotlight on her fragile emotional state. And that she could not risk—in case Ash looked again, and saw too much.

So, she thought reluctantly, it was far better to sing with good grace and have done with it.

She let him play the melody, then came in with the reprise, her voice warm and strong. '*"Plaisir d'amour ne dure qu'un moment, Chagrin d'amour dure toute la vie".*'

She sang the whole thing through in French, her own inner sadness and regret lending a whole new depth of emotion to her performance, then repeated the plangent melancholy refrain one last time in English. '"The joys of love are but a moment long, The pain of love endures the whole life long".'

It was, she thought, as she allowed the final syllables to linger on the night air, a reminder worth repeating.

When she'd finished there was a silence, then Laurent said, 'That was wonderful.' He turned to Ash. 'Didn't you think so, *mon ami*?'

'Beautiful.' He looked at Chellie, his mouth twisting faintly. 'Although it wasn't quite what I had in mind. Those are fairly negative sentiments.'

'Negative,' she said. 'Or realistic, perhaps.' She gave a slight shrug. 'Everyone has to make their own interpretation—choose for themselves.'

'So, what side of the fence do you come down on, Michelle?' The question was put lightly but his eyes were intense, fixed on hers. A hungry gaze, she realised. Warning her that he was asking far more than his words suggested at face value.

Telling her without equivocation that her answer would decide whether or not she would spend the night in his arms.

The joys of love are but a moment long. The line still sang in her mind, with its chilling emphasis that, however passionate or miraculous that moment might be, it could not last. And that, if she surrendered to it, an eternity of loneliness might follow. Something she could not afford to forget.

Chellie lifted her chin. She said, quietly and clearly, 'That's quite simple. I choose not to be unhappy for the rest of my life.'

She forced her mouth into the semblance of a smile. 'And now, if you'll excuse me, I'll wish you both goodnight.'

She walked away with her head held high, and without hurrying or glancing back. But at the bottom of the companionway she stopped, leaning shakily against the wall, pressing a hand to her trembling mouth.

'Oh, God,' she whispered. 'How long am I going to be able to carry on pretending?'

Up in the wheelhouse there was a heavy silence which Laurent eventually broke, his voice quiet. 'You have a real problem, *mon ami*.'

Dull colour spread across Ash's cheekbones. He reached for another cheroot. Lit it. 'Nothing I can't handle.'

'First handle Victor,' Laurent said shortly. 'Explain to him why you have decided to keep the girl on St Hilaire instead of taking her back to England, as instructed. And see how near you come to the truth, *hein*?' he added with dry emphasis.

Ash dealt with Victor and his concerns in one succinct phrase.

'I made it clear from the start that the final negotiations would be conducted on my own territory,' he added curtly.

Laurent gave him a level look. 'Unfortunately Sir Clive Greer does not wish to come halfway across the world to make the payment and collect his daughter—and he is not a man used to having his wishes disregarded.'

Ash shrugged. 'He can take it or leave it. Just as long as he pays us the agreed amount.'

Laurent stared at him. 'You are still saying this is just about money?'

Ash drew deeply on the cheroot. 'Of course,' he said. 'What else?'

'Then why keep her with you instead of taking the next flight from St Vincent or Barbados?'

'Because in a situation like this, he's the obvious one for her to turn to,' Ash said. 'Yet she's never even mentioned him. Admitted he's her father.' His mouth tightened. 'Don't you find that strange?'

Laurent gave him a cynical look. 'He is buying her back. That is all you need to know. And it is clear that he already regards her as damaged goods,' he added, his mouth twisting in distaste. 'So beware of making a bad situation worse.'

'Why?' Ash stubbed out the cheroot with sudden violence. 'Because he may reduce the price?'

'And you said it was just the money.' Laurent shook his head as he began to collect the used crockery together. 'I think you are fooling yourself, *mon vieux*.'

Ash glared at him. 'When I need your advice, I'll ask for it.'

Laurent grinned back. 'Life is too short, I think,' he said, and began to hum *'Plaisir d'Amour'* softly under his breath.

Chellie sat on the edge of the bed, head bent, fingers almost convulsively gripping the edge of the mattress.

She'd done the right thing, she told herself with harsh vehemence. The sensible thing. The *only* thing.

She'd made it crystal-clear to Ash that she intended to hold him at arm's length for the remainder of their acquaintance. However long that might be.

Two days, she thought, if she was lucky. If the consul turned out to be co-operative and helpful, and actually believed her unlikely story. And then she would be on her way out of Ash's life for ever.

But going where?

That was something she hadn't yet thought through with any clarity. The present had been occupying her mind too fully to spare much time for the future.

But she'd made a start by accepting that Ash could never be part of it, for so many reasons.

He was very much an enigma, she thought, and that in itself carried its own kind of glamour. And he'd saved her, and she would always be grateful for that. So maybe that was all there was to it—and one day she would only remember the gratitude and dismiss the rest as a passing fancy.

But now she had to concentrate on the rest of her life. Galling as it was, it was clear she had little choice but to return to England. She needed access to money, and although the money from her late mother's legacy only brought in a modest income, it would support her until she could find work of some kind. And a bedsit, too. She could no longer afford her old flat.

Besides, by this time Ramon would probably have run up astronomical bills on her credit cards, and she would have to deal with that.

She would also need to get some qualifications. Becoming a professional singer was beyond her reach, but a catering course would be useful, she thought slowly, although she was cancelling her original wild idea of working on boats. Dry land would be much safer. Or maybe she would learn computing skills.

She sighed soundlessly. The outlook seemed pretty bleak. She'd been taught a very costly lesson in the past weeks—but the financial implications were the least of it. And somehow she would have to deal with that. Somehow.

But first and foremost she had to tackle the consul—get him on her side. Because she didn't want to contemplate what might happen if he refused to help. And they were not always sympathetic to people turning up on their doorstep without means.

I should have to turn to Ash again, she thought, her heart missing a painful beat. I'd have no choice. I can't count on some other saviour coming to my rescue.

She slid off the bed and began to undress, her mind still going in weary circles.

She would have to borrow some more clothes, of course. That was unavoidable. She couldn't visit the consul wearing a crumpled denim skirt or Mama Rita's black dress, not if she wanted to be taken seriously.

Some underwear, a pair of cotton trousers and a couple of tops should be enough, she thought, replacing the crimson blouse and skirt on their hanger and touching their silky folds with a rueful hand. Emergency rations from now on.

And she would have to find some way of compensating

her unknown benefactress, too, for the unrestricted access to her wardrobe.

Although she probably won't miss any of the stuff I've used, Chellie thought with a faint shrug. Most of it seems to be brand-new. I expect she has a new selection in every port.

But she'd return what she could, she decided—washed, ironed and pristine.

She took another quick shower, then cleansed and toned her face, and ran a brush through her hair before reaching for her nightgown.

And paused, looking at her naked reflection in the mirror, seeing herself for the first time as an object of desire in a man's eyes. Remembering, with a sharp indrawn breath, how Ash had stared at her, his gaze urgent—demanding. Wanting her.

No one, she thought, had ever looked at her in quite that way before. And maybe no one would ever again.

And she'd rejected him. She closed her eyes, pressing her clenched fist against her mouth. She'd gone for the wise, brave option. Obeyed her mind and not the unbidden, uncontrollable clamour in her flesh.

But would Ash accept her no for an answer? Or would he choose instead to come and find her—and take—because he knew that was what she really wanted...?

She could not be dishonest with herself any longer.

There was a flask of her favourite scent among the toiletries in the bathroom. Chellie found herself almost dreamily touching the crystal stopper to her throat, her breasts, the curve of her elbows and her thighs.

She picked up the lip-lustre she'd used earlier and softened the lines of her mouth with colour.

The girl looking back at her from the mirror seemed totally alien, her bare skin faintly flushed, her eyes wide and drowsy with expectancy and her mouth curving into a slow smile.

She breathed the cloud of fragrance rising from her warm

flesh, and the older, muskier scent that she realised was intermingled with it. A scent that was totally wanton—and wholly female.

There was an ache in her breasts, their rosy peaks already jutting in excitement. A soft, sensual throb that was echoed deep inside her and yearned to be assuaged.

She was a woman at last—ready and eager for her lover.

He will come to me, she thought. He must…

She went softly to the door and drew back the little bolt she had fastened earlier. She extinguished all the lights except the small shaded lamp beside the bed.

Then she slid under the covers, drawing the sheet loosely up to her hips, and settled back against the pillows to wait for him.

It was his own choice now, she thought. All he had to do was tap at the door, and she would say his name and open her arms to welcome him.

She measured out the time by the pace of her own heartbeat. Was it really so agonisingly slow?

And when at last she heard his footsteps, descending the companionway and approaching down the passage, her heart seemed to stop beating altogether.

She swallowed, her eyes fixed on the door, listening—hoping for his knock.

She heard him slow—come to a halt outside her door. There was a silence—endless—brooding—and she wanted to call out to him, but her taut throat muscles refused to obey her.

She heard a faint noise, saw the doorhandle turn slightly. Her entire body tensed in a mixture of nervousness and longing as she waited for the door to open.

But it remained where it was, and a moment later she realised the handle had been gently released again.

Then she heard him going away from her, his footsteps fading, and presently the sound of his own door shutting with an awful finality.

She knew then that he would not return. That she would spend the night alone. And she turned over, burying her face in the pillow, her body as rigid and as cold as a stone.

And, presently, she wept.

CHAPTER SEVEN

CHELLIE awoke early the following morning and lay for a while, looking out at the cloudless sky. The storm of tears that had assailed her the previous night had left her feeling drained of all emotion. At one point she had even been forced to stuff the corner of the pillow into her mouth to muffle the harsh sobs that were tearing through her, terrified that they might be heard. And eventually, she supposed, she must have fallen into an exhausted sleep.

She could remember brief, uneasy dreams, but none of them had left any lasting trace.

And now it was the next day, reality once more. All dreams must be forgotten. She had to get up and repair the ravages, and pretend that everything was fine.

Maybe I should take up acting as a career, she thought with a grimace as she pushed back the sheet and got out of bed.

The scent she had applied with such hope last night still lingered on her skin, making her feel vaguely nauseated. She knew she would never wear it again.

She looked pale, she thought critically, catching sight of herself in the mirror, and her eyes felt bruised, but apart from that she appeared relatively together. Her face would not give away any secrets.

She showered rapidly, and dressed in pale pink linen shorts and a matching camisole top. Then she made her way straight to the galley, reviewing all the information that Laurent had passed on yesterday.

Today, the bread was cut precisely, and toasted evenly, the coffee was strong and aromatic, and the eggs boiled for four minutes only. She gave a nod of satisfaction as she rang the bell.

She was setting the food on the table in the saloon when Ash appeared, wearing a pair of frayed denim shorts. He halted in the doorway, the blue eyes narrowed slightly as he studied her.

Chellie met his gaze, her smile deliberately cool and non-committal.

He said slowly, 'You're an early riser.' He paused. 'Couldn't you sleep?'

'Just as soon as my head hit the pillow,' Chellie lied. 'But after the trouble I got into yesterday I thought I'd better make a prompt start today.' She gave a light laugh. 'After all, I don't want to be keel-hauled at this stage of the voyage.'

Ash's brows lifted as he surveyed the table. 'It all looks— wonderful. You amaze me.'

'It's not really very astonishing.' Chellie poured coffee with a steady hand and handed him the cup. She added quietly, 'I try never to make the same stupid mistake twice, that's all.' She let that sink into the silence, then picked up the waiting tray. 'I'll take Laurent's food up to him.'

'No,' he said. 'I'll do that. You stay here and have your breakfast. I'll be straight back.' He paused. 'I think we need to talk.'

Alone, Chellie sank down on to a chair, aware that her mouth was dry and her legs were trembling under her. She took a gulp of chilled pineapple juice.

Talk? she thought desperately. What could he possibly want to talk about? Especially when she was so anxious to avoid any kind of tête-à-tête?

She wondered with sudden dread if he had come back to her door after all the previous night, and heard her weeping.

What am I going to say to him if so? she asked herself frantically. How can I possibly explain?

The worst-case scenario was that he intended to tell her

why he'd had second thoughts and walked away from her last night.

Because, however reasoned his explanation, she wasn't sure that she could bear to hear it. Knowing there was no place for her in his life was one thing. Hearing it from his own lips quite another.

Supposing her emotions got the better of her all over again?

'Oh, God,' she whispered to herself. That would be the ultimate humiliation. To weep for his favours in front of him.

And she couldn't let him arrive back and find her sitting like a bump on a log, staring at the food, either, she told herself with renewed determination. Somehow she had to make herself eat something, and do it with every sign of appetite and enjoyment. Everything normal in this best of all possible worlds.

She poured herself coffee, took a heartening swig, then cut the top off her egg and reached for a slice of toast.

'I started without you,' she said brightly as Ash returned and took a seat opposite her. 'I hope you don't mind?'

'Not at all,' he said politely. 'You may find this hard to believe, but I'm really quite tolerant.'

'I'll try to remember.' She forced down another spoonful of egg.

There was a pause, then he said, 'Laurent has been very complimentary about your French accent'

'Oh.' She flushed. 'That's—kind of him.'

'It's a pity we'll be at St Hilaire so soon,' he went on. 'Or you might have revealed even more hidden talents.'

'I doubt that,' Chellie returned shortly. 'I can sing and speak French. That doesn't amount to much.'

'And you can dance, too,' he said. 'We mustn't forget that,' he added silkily, a disturbing glint in his eyes. 'Even if the performance was a little—curtailed.'

Her face warmed. 'I'd prefer not to be reminded of that—any of it.'

'Well, there we differ,' he said, shrugging. 'Because it will always remain one of my most cherished memories.' He paused. 'So, where did you learn to speak French so well?'

Chellie hesitated. 'My mother was French,' she revealed reluctantly.

'Ah,' he said. 'Then that would explain ''Michelle''.'

She shook her head. 'Not exactly. I was named for my grandfather. He died just before I was born. Otherwise…'

Her voice faltered into silence, and Ash sent her a keen glance.

'Yes?' he prompted.

She stared down at her plate. 'Otherwise my father would never have agreed,' she said slowly, angry with herself for revealing so much. 'He always hated the name and had wanted me to be christened Elizabeth. In fact, that's what he started calling me after my mother died, until he was eventually persuaded it wasn't a good idea.'

He said lightly, 'A man of strong will. Who managed to talk him round?'

'My nanny,' she said. 'Our family doctor. My aunt Margaret.' She shrugged. 'Anyway, it doesn't really matter. It was all a long time ago.'

'Yet you've remembered it?'

She thought, *Oh, I remember more than that. The way he tried to remove every trace of my mother from the house, as if she'd never existed, or as if he'd demeaned himself by marrying a girl who was a foreigner and who'd worked as a cabaret singer. The way he tried to stifle my own interest in music.*

'Some things tend to stick.' She made her voice dismissive. 'Is that all you wanted to know?'

'It's not even a fraction of it,' Ash drawled, pouring himself more coffee.

'However, it's all I'm prepared to say on the subject.' She drew a breath. 'Now, may I ask a question? What time will we reach St Hilaire?'

'Early afternoon.'

'I see.' Chellie bit her lip. 'And you're quite sure I can't reach the consul over the weekend?'

'Don't even try,' he advised lazily. 'Not if you want him on your side. Anyway, what's the hurry?'

'It clearly hasn't occurred to you,' Chellie said tautly, 'that I might want to get on with the rest of my life.'

'No,' he admitted. 'I wasn't even aware you knew what form it was going to take.' He leaned back in his seat, eyelids drooping as he studied her. 'So, what do you have in mind?'

'That,' she said, 'is none of your damned business.'

'Wrong,' he said. 'According to the old saying, if you save someone's skin, then they belong to you for evermore. So I have a vested interest in your future, songbird. Not to mention that pretty hide of yours,' he added mockingly.

Chellie set her jaw. 'Until you get tired of playing Galahad, anyway,' she said stonily.

'I am not playing anything, Michelle.' Ash sounded weary. 'In fact, I'm bloody serious. So may we please stop fencing and start talking some sense?'

She flushed. 'Very well,' she said constrictedly. 'If we must.'

'Where do you intend to go after St Hilaire? Home?'

She hesitated. 'I have no home—in that sense. But I'll head for London, I suppose. I—know people there. There'll be someone I can stay with while I sort myself out.'

'My God,' he said.

'You don't approve?' She tilted her chin in challenge.

'I've had nightmares I've enjoyed more,' he said shortly.

'I've been staying with you,' Chellie objected. 'And you're a complete stranger.'

'How odd you should think that,' he said softly. 'When I feel as if I've known you all my life.'

Her throat tightened, making breathing difficult. The words seemed to hover in the air between them, but she couldn't think of a single comeback, or even meet his gaze.

So she busied herself instead with collecting up the used crockery.

Eventually he spoke again. 'Is someone else's sofa your only scheme?'

'At the moment. But please don't concern yourself. I'd be going to friends, you know.'

His brows lifted. 'Are these the same friends that allowed you to run away with your con-man boyfriend?'

She piled the dishes on to a tray. 'I didn't really tell them about Ramon. Certainly not what we were planning. I didn't mention that to anyone.'

'Why all the secrecy?'

She thought, *Because I was scared that word would somehow get back to my father and he'd find a way of stopping me. After all, he always had before...*

She shrugged. 'Up to then my life had been an open book,' she countered. 'I enjoyed having something to hide for once.' She paused. 'Besides, Ramon never really wanted to meet my friends.' She pulled a face. 'He said that he only wanted to be with me, not other people.'

'How sweet and caring of him,' Ash drawled.

'I thought so then,' Chellie returned, carrying the tray into the galley. 'But I won't be so naïve in future. I'll keep reminding myself that everyone has a hidden agenda.'

'That doesn't bode well for future relationships.'

Chellie was uneasily aware that he'd followed her and was standing only a couple of feet away, arms folded, leaning against the worktop.

'I'm not planning to have any.' She shrugged a casual shoulder. 'I intend to savour my independence.'

'I hear the words, songbird,' he said softly. 'But I'm not convinced. That beautiful bottom lip of yours is much too soft and generous for such a hardline attitude. One day you'll want to share your kisses—and your life.'

'And set myself up for another disappointment?' Her tone was suddenly ragged as she remembered last night—how she'd stared across at the door, her whole body aching with the consciousness of his presence on the other side of it. How she'd yearned—prayed for it to open. And how he'd left her, torn apart with longing and frustration and totally bereft.

She shook her head. 'I don't think so.'

There was an odd silence, then he said, 'I didn't realise that he'd got to you quite so deeply. I'm—sorry. But not all men are like Ramon. You'll learn to trust again, Michelle. I promise you will.'

'You should write a magazine column.' She kept her tone light and mocking. '"Advice for the dumped-on". As for promises,' she added casually. 'Just guarantee to get me to the consul on St Hilaire first thing on Monday morning and I'll be completely happy.'

'You think so?' he asked with sudden harshness. 'I say you're wrong, Michelle. In fact, right now, I doubt if you'll ever discover the true meaning of the word as long as you live.'

And he walked away, leaving her standing there, staring after him in shocked silence.

The road ran dizzyingly along the coast, allowing Chellie tantalising glimpses, through the clustering palm trees which fringed it, of silver beaches below and a sea shifting endlessly from shades of emerald to turquoise, through all the colours in between.

Not that she had much opportunity to be entranced. She was more preoccupied with retaining her seat in the Jeep that was taking her—somewhere.

The driver, Alphonse, was a cheerful soul with a wide grin, who whistled and hummed snatches of song while he drove.

She'd asked him in English and French where exactly they were heading, but had been answered with only a smiling shrug and a 'Not far,' which told her nothing.

She supposed the sensible course would have been to find out her eventual destination before getting into this bone-shaking vehicle and being jolted over roads little better than cart tracks in places, while she clung, white-knuckled, to the side of the Jeep.

But then, from what she'd seen so far, carts seemed to be the preferred form of transport.

Besides, she'd been so relieved to find that Ash was not coming with her that all other considerations had paled into insignificance.

Her last hours on board *La Belle Rêve* had not been easy. She had been at pains to keep out of Ash's way. She'd felt too raw and confused to risk another confrontation so soon. And he had seemed equally keen to avoid her.

Fortunately the approach to St Hilaire had provided a new focus, and she'd hung over the rail, scanning its high and rocky hinterland with genuine interest.

Laurent had come to lean beside her with a sigh of quiet satisfaction. 'Home at last.' He pointed to the tallest peak. 'That is L'Aiguille,' he told her. 'The Needle—our volcano. It is thanks to her and her little sisters around her, Les Epingles, that our island is so fertile and our crops grow so well.'

'Volcano?' Chellie repeated in a hollow voice. 'Is it dangerous?'

Laurent gave her a teasing glance. 'It is not considered in a fatal phase,' he said solemnly. 'You may climb up to the crater and inspect it for yourself, if you wish.'

She forced a smile. 'I think I'll pass. Besides, I won't really be around long enough for any sightseeing. I want to be on my way as soon as possible.'

'As soon as possible?' Laurent mused, and shook his head. 'I don't think we have a phrase for that in these islands.'

She laughed, then became aware that Ash was watching and moved away, going down to her stateroom. She packed a few judiciously chosen items from the closet and drawers into her bag, then changed into a cream linen dress, ornamented down the front by large black buttons, and slid her feet into low-heeled black pumps.

When she met the consul she needed to look like someone merely suffering from temporary financial embarrassment, she thought, rather than some pathetic waif or stray. And this outfit, by one of her own favourite designers, should do the trick.

They anchored in the middle of St Hilaire's surprisingly large harbour, and a launch arrived with promptitude to take them to shore.

Chellie couldn't help noticing that while Laurent was greeted with laughter and uproarious slaps on the back, Ash was treated with smiling respect, triggering all sorts of questions in her mind.

Questions, as she reminded herself, which were never likely to be answered.

As she stood hesitantly on the quayside, Laurent came over to her. 'Mam'selle Chellie.' He took her hand. 'I wish you *au revoir*. I look forward to hearing that you have become a great singer when we meet again.'

Unlikely on both counts, Chellie thought, as she smiled and murmured something non-committal.

She looked around, noting how the low red-roofed houses clung to the steep hillside above her in charmingly haphazard fashion. Confronting her was a row of warehouses, brightly painted, and there were a number of stalls offering fruit, vegetables, pottery and woven baskets.

'Your room's all arranged.' Ash appeared suddenly beside her, making her jump. 'I'm sorry I can't accompany you,' he added, without the least sign of regret. 'But I have things to do. Alphonse, here, will deliver you in perfect safety.' He signalled, and a tall, rangy man climbed down from the Jeep and took Chellie's bag for her.

Ash added no further explanation, wished her a perfunctory goodbye, and turned away.

And that, she told herself with a certain defiance as she got in the Jeep, was exactly—absolutely—what she wanted.

I have to stop thinking about him, she told herself forcefully as they drove off. Or I'm going to go mad. We've said goodbye, and now I'm on my own, in charge of my own destiny. I need to concentrate on that. Focus on the rest of my life—and taking the next step towards it.

She'd expected to be driven straight to some small hotel in St Hilaire itself, but the capital was long behind them now, and still the Jeep lurched on its precarious way.

In spite of her attempt at positive thinking, there was a rawness deep inside her, and an odd sense of disorientation, not lessened by this unexpected journey.

She could only imagine they were destined for some secluded tourist resort in an exclusive corner of the island, and while the idea of some rest and relaxation beckoned seductively, it wasn't really convenient to be marooned so far from the hub of the capital. Especially, she thought broodingly, when she needed to present herself at the consular office first thing on Monday morning.

Perhaps that consideration had slipped Ash's mind, but she didn't think so. He didn't strike her as someone who forgot much. Or nothing, anyway, that he wanted to remember…

But then what did she know? He'd revealed so little of himself during their brief time together that he was still a cross between an enigma and a chameleon. Always changing, she thought with a stifled sigh, like the restless sea beneath the cliffs.

And paused, her hand flying in shock to her mouth as she too remembered something.

My passport, she thought, horrified. Oh, God, he still has it.

She turned to Alphonse. She said in French, 'We must go back to the town. Find Monsieur Brennan. It is very important. A matter of life and death.'

But Alphonse merely grinned at her, said something that was apparently meant to be soothing in some incomprehensible local *patois*, and drove on.

She tried again. 'No, you must turn round. I really need to go back.'

For a moment she thought he was going to do as he asked, because he turned the wheel suddenly, swinging the Jeep across the road almost at a right angle and startling a small yelp from her.

But, instead of completing the expected U-turn, he left the coast road altogether, taking a narrow dusty track that Chellie had not even noticed was there, and she found herself being driven downhill between tall hibiscus hedges.

'Where are we?' she demanded breathlessly, and Alphonse pointed ahead to a wooden archway, with the single word 'Arcadie' carved into its overhead timbers.

I suppose that's meant to convey something, Chellie thought with rising vexation. When am I going to start getting some straight answers round here?

They seemed to be descending into a steep valley, plunging into a green tunnel where overhanging foliage almost blocked out the sun. Through the trees, she could just glimpse the lines of a tiled roof.

Clinging on like grim death, as the Jeep lurched and bounced, she gasped out, 'Is that the hotel—the place where you're taking me?'

Alphonse flashed her a grin. *'Oui, mademoiselle. C'est Arcadie.'*

'But I won't be able to stay there.' She tried to speak clearly and concisely above the roar of the engine. 'I'll need my passport to register, and Mr Brennan has it. He forgot to give it to me and I have to get it back. Do you understand?'

Alphonse nodded, still smiling, and drove on without slackening his pace by one iota.

Nuts, Chellie told herself helplessly. He must be. I'm driving round with the local fruitcake.

And if the building below was a hotel, it was a pretty small one, she thought, a frown creasing her brow. There could be supplementary cabins dotted round the grounds, but so far she hadn't spotted any sign of them.

Nor could she see any flash of blue water suggesting that Hotel Arcadie boasted a swimming pool, and that was a disappointment. St Hilaire might not be a leader in the Caribbean tourist industry, but surely whatever hotels it possessed should be expected to have the usual amenities.

And, she realised, she'd been looking forward to a swim.

In her old life in London, swimming had been one of her favourite forms of exercise—apart from dancing. In the pool near her home she'd swum in the early morning, pushing herself almost to the limit of exhaustion. Distancing herself from the devils of boredom and frustration that had plagued her so often.

Here, she had other frustrations to work through—other demons to exorcise—and the prospect of stretching her limbs in cool water—restoring her body to fitness—had been irresistible.

A cold shower wouldn't be the same thing at all, she thought wryly. That was, of course, if the hotel was sophisticated enough to have bathrooms. She didn't even know that for certain.

But when they eventually emerged from the overhanging trees into full sunlight, and she was able to take her first proper look at Arcadie, she had to admit that she'd been unfair. Because it certainly lived up to its name.

It was a gracious two-storey building, standing square and painted white, its roof tiled in faded terracotta. It was surrounded by well-kept lawns of coarse grass and flowerbeds that were a sheer riot of colour.

A shady verandah encircled the ground floor, guarding long shuttered windows, and a balcony with a wooden balustrade surrounded the first floor.

It was very still, only the harsh cry of a bird breaking the welcome silence as the Jeep stopped.

Chellie saw that the main door was open, and an elderly

man with grizzled hair stood waiting in the shade of the pillared portico.

He came forward and opened the passenger door, lifting down Chellie's bag and offering her a hand to assist her descent.

'*Mademoiselle.*' He wore dark trousers and a pristine white linen coat, and his smile was grave and polite. 'My name is Cornelius. Welcome to Arcadie.'

Chellie got down stiffly, resisting the temptation to rub the bits that ached from that headlong journey. She felt hot and sticky, and was aware that the dress she'd worn to impress was creased and dusty.

She took a deep breath. 'I'm sorry, but there's been a mistake,' she began, then whirled round, gasping, as the Jeep's engine roared into life again and the vehicle took off in another swirl of dust, with a cheery backward wave from Alphonse.

'Hell's bells.' Ridiculously, she tried to run after it. 'Don't go,' she yelled. '*Ne me quittez pas.* You can't leave me stranded here. You *can't...*'

'You must not disturb yourself, *mademoiselle.*' Cornelius's voice was soothing as he came to her side. He took her arm and began to urge her gently but firmly towards the door. 'All is well, and you are quite safe. I will show you your room, then Rosalie, my wife, will make you some iced tea.'

Chellie stared at him. 'If you're the owner, then there's something you should know,' she said, swallowing. 'I've been brought here under false pretences. You see, I've no passport or money either, and I needed the driver to take me back to town so that I could sort something out.'

'Neither are required, *mademoiselle.* And I am not the owner of Arcadie, merely an employee. Whereas you, of course, are an honoured guest.'

They were inside now, in a spacious hall kept cool by the gentle movement of a ceiling fan. The walls were painted ivory, and the floor had been constructed from some wood the colour of warm honey.

Apart from a carved wooden chest supporting a ceramic bowl heavy with blue and crimson flowers, the hall was empty. There was no sign of a reception desk, or any of the other paraphernalia of hotel life.

Just a wide curving flight of stairs in the same honeyed wood—which she was being encouraged towards, she realised.

She hung back. 'It's very—quiet. So, how many more are there? Honoured guests, I mean?'

'As yet, you are the only one, Mademoiselle Greer.'

'I see.' It wasn't true, but there seemed little point in hanging around arguing the point, so she followed Cornelius up the stairs, the polished banister smooth under her hand. The only touch of reality in a confusing world, she thought.

She said, 'Has the hotel only just opened for business, then?'

'Hotel?' Cornelius halted, glancing back at her in obvious astonishment. 'Arcadie is a private house, *mademoiselle*. You are here at the invitation of the owner, Mist' Howard.'

Chellie's hand tightened on the rail. 'But there must be some mistake,' she said, trying to speak calmly. 'I don't know any such person. Is he here? I—I'd better speak to him at once...'

'I regret—Mist' Howard is in America.'

'In America?' she repeated, stunned. 'Then how could he...?' Her voice tailed away as realisation began to dawn.

'Ah,' she said softly, between her teeth. 'I think I understand.'

So this was the arrangement Ash Brennan had made, she thought smouldering. Once more he was presuming on his employer's good nature, it seemed. He must be awfully sure of his position in the family to take such advantage. But then he was going to be his boss's son in law—wasn't he?

She forced a smile. 'Tell me, Cornelius, does your Mr Howard own a boat called *La Belle Rêve*,' by any chance?'

'*Mais, bien sûr, mademoiselle.*' He gave her an anxious look. 'There is a problem? You still wish to leave?'

'No, not at all.' Chellie gave an airy shrug. 'Why shouldn't I stay in his house? After all, I've enjoyed so much of his hospitality already in the last few days.' She ticked off on her fingers. 'I've sailed on his boat, eaten his food, and I'm even wearing his daughter's clothes, so what does one more thing matter?' She paused again. 'I presume he *does* have a daughter?' She tried to make her voice casual.

Cornelius nodded. 'Indeed, *mademoiselle.*' There was fondness in his tone. 'Mademoiselle Julie is with him in Florida.'

'How delightful,' Chellie said brightly. 'All the same, I hope I'm not sleeping in her room. I should hate her to arrive and find it occupied.' In fact, I should hate her to arrive, period, she added silently, her memory serving up the image of the smiling blonde in the photograph.

'You have been given the guest suite, *mademoiselle.*' Cornelius sounded faintly shocked. 'But neither Mist' Howard or *Mam'selle* are expected.'

Good, thought Chellie, and meant it.

But, in spite of her misgivings, she could not help but be enchanted by her accommodation. An airy sitting room, furnished with a brightly cushioned rattan sofa and chairs, opened into a large bedroom, with soft turquoise walls and filmy white drapes billowing gently in the faint breeze from the open window.

The low, wide bed had a quilted coverlet, patterned in shades of turquoise and white, and the ivory and gold tiled bathroom held a deep tub, as well as a walk-in shower with glass screens.

Chellie was suddenly aware that tears were not far away. All this comfort—all this beauty, she thought, for someone frankly fraying at the edges.

She said huskily, 'It—it's wonderful, Cornelius. Thank you.'

He inclined his head, looking pleased. He said, 'If you give your dress to Rosalie, *mademoiselle*, she will have it laundered for you.'

Of course, she thought, as the door closed behind him. As her father's daughter, this was the kind of service she had been taught to expect. Yet she'd never really appreciated it until this moment.

She stripped, and had a long, luxurious shower, hoping to wash away the blues, then changed into a pair of cream cut-offs and a black vest top. She slipped on a pair of light canvas shoes, and ventured downstairs.

A large woman in a striped cotton dress came surging to meet her, the dark eyes flicking over Chellie in a swift, shrewd assessment that in no way detracted from the warmth of her smile.

'You would like some refreshment, *mademoiselle*—iced tea, or maybe pineapple juice?' She whisked Chellie through a sitting room replete with large squashy sofas and low tables, and out through sliding glass doors to the verandah at the back of the house, where a table and chairs had been set and a tray awaited, set with covered jugs and glasses.

'It looks lovely,' Chellie said, with a little sigh of pleasure. 'May I have some tea, please?'

She watched as Rosalie poured the tea with a satisfying clink of ice cubes, and took the glass she was offered.

One sip convinced her that it was the best iced tea she'd ever tasted, full of flavour and not too sweet, and so she told Rosalie, who looked quietly gratified.

Encouraged by this, Chellie decided on another tack. 'It's good of you to go to all this trouble,' she said. 'After all, it can't have been convenient to have me dumped on you at such short notice.' She paused. 'I thought Mr Brennan was sending me to a hotel.'

Rosalie dismissed all hotels with a wave of her hand, lips pursed disapprovingly. 'You are Mist' Ash's friend, *mam'selle*, so where else would you stay? Mr Howard would wish you to be here.'

Would he? I wonder, Chellie thought, her own mouth twisting. And is that really what I am—Ash's friend? He wasn't very friendly when we parted.

Which reminded her. She said 'Rosalie, I need to contact Mr Ash fairly urgently. Would it be possible for me to call him on the telephone in St Hilaire?'

'Mist' Ash?' the older woman repeated, setting the jug back on the tray and arranging its beaded muslin cover with minute care. She shook her head. 'I don't know, *mam'selle*. Don't know where he might be.'

'But it isn't a huge place,' Chellie protested. 'Surely you must be able to reach him somewhere.'

Rosalie folded her hands in front of her. 'It's not easy, *mam'selle*. But I ask Cornelius,' she added with the air of one making a major concession.

Chellie sighed in silent perplexity as Rosalie went back into the house. Another dead end, it seemed. Or was she being deliberately blocked? Surely not. Yet Laurent had indicated that Ash had his own place on the island, which must mean an address—a phone number.

Unless he'd given instructions that he wasn't to be contacted—particularly by her. Maybe he'd decided it was time to draw a line, once and for all, under this strange stop-go relationship.

Shaking off the faint feeling of desolation assailing her, she settled herself back against the cushions of her wicker lounger and drank some more tea. A climbing plant, heavy with blossom, was spilling over the balustrade, and a huge butterfly with pale velvety wings was busy among the flowers.

There was a flash of green and gold, and a parrot flew across the grass and vanished into a nearby tree.

Arcadia indeed, she thought, drawing a swift, delighted breath. But she could not allow herself to relax and enjoy it too much. Her presence here was a strictly temporary measure, and she must never forget it.

Another twenty-four hours and I'll be gone, she told herself, and all this will be behind me. And perhaps then I can start to forget—and to heal. And she sighed again, wishing with all her heart that she could believe that.

CHAPTER EIGHT

AT THE time it had seemed like a good idea to go for a stroll. To explore Arcadie beyond the immediate confines of the garden.

Now, with the sun baking on her back, an escort of persistent insects, and an apparently impenetrable wall of greenery in front of her, Chellie was having second thoughts.

But she'd needed to do something, she argued as she pushed forward, parting the thick, fleshy leaves that impeded her, looking for the track which she'd been following but seemed to have temporarily mislaid.

Oh, come on, she told herself impatiently. It's here somewhere. It has to be.

It would have been much easier to stay on the verandah, drinking more tea and finishing the plate of tiny cinammon biscuits that Rosalie had supplied along with it.

But she would only have started to brood—to let her thoughts take her down paths even more hazardous than the one she was now embarked on, which seemed to have led her into the middle of a rainforest.

And over it all hung the mountain. Not the Needle itself, but one of the smaller Pins, yet composed of grey volcanic rock just the same.

It took guts to make a home in such a place, she thought. It was so beautiful, but so savage and unpredictable at the same time.

Someone had once said that volcanoes never really died, but merely slept, and she could only hope that they were wrong.

She found herself almost regretting that she would never

meet Mr Howard, the intrepid man who'd built his house here, daring the dark gods of hurricanes and seismic upheavals to do their worst.

Beyond the tailored lawns round the house the wilderness waited, primitive and still untamed. And she should not be taking any more risks here. She'd undergone enough ordeals lately to last her a lifetime. Now she really needed to step back into civilisation and stay there.

I should turn back, she thought. So why don't I?

Well, for one thing, the walk might do her good. It might even encourage her appetite too. Rosalie had told her when she came for the tray that dinner would be at eight-thirty, and she looked like a woman who took her cooking seriously, and would insist on it being shown due respect.

But at the moment Chellie felt too edgy for hunger. Because Rosalie had also brought the unwelcome news that neither she nor Cornelius had a number where Ash could be reached. *Impasse*.

Arcadie was a beautiful house, and its valley setting was spectacular, but it was in the middle of nowhere.

No one asked me, she thought restively, if I wished to be cut off from the known world. At the moment, my only way out of here is to walk. There are no locks or bolts, but I feel like a prisoner just the same.

But now, like a ray of hope, here was the track again, and somewhere ahead of her, she thought, frowning, was the unmistakable splash of water.

She walked carefully, trying not to twist her ankle on the thick roots which made every step a hazard. She ducked under an overhanging branch, straightened, then stood openmouthed, staring in delight at the scene in front of her.

Her ears had not deceived her. The little waterfall she'd heard sprang straight from the grey rock, spilling some ten feet into a deep natural basin, yet barely ruffling its surface.

Here at last was the swimming pool she'd longed for. And it must be safe, because someone had constructed a small diving board, which waited invitingly. Almost beckoning to her.

One of the accompanying insects grazed her skin, and she brushed it aside impatiently, her eyes fixed on the sky and the light puffs of cloud reflected back by the clear water. Already imagining its caress.

She could, of course, go back to the house and fetch the solitary swimsuit she'd brought with her.

On the other hand...

Impulsively, she kicked off her shoes, then stripped off the vest top, dropping it on to the slab of flat rock beside the diving board. She peeled down the cotton pants, and the lacy briefs she wore beneath them, then walked to the end of the board, positioned herself, and dived in.

The water felt tinglingly fresh and cold against her overheated skin. She let herself go down into the seemingly endless depths, then kicked for the surface, coming up, gasping and laughing, into the sunlight.

She'd never swum naked before, and found herself almost guiltily relishing the intensity of the sensation.

She plunged briefly again, then began to swim in earnest, her body instinctively finding its own smooth rhythm, her muscles working in co-ordination against the strong pull of the water.

Oh, but she'd missed this, she thought, as eventually she twisted sinuously on to her back and floated, staring up at the blue arc of the sky. For the first time in many weeks she felt almost at peace with herself.

If ever I have a boat of my own, she thought, I'll call it *Naiad* in memory of this afternoon.

It was ludicrous in her situation to make any kind of plan, but she had to be optimistic, imagine a future where she was in control and prospering. And owning a boat...

Everyone needs something to aim for, she told herself.

She swam slowly over to the waterfall and pulled herself up on to the slippery rock at its base. She stood upright under the cascade and lifted her face to the pouring water, revelling at the sting of it against her skin, the cold lash of the torrent driving at her stomach and thighs, urgent against her breasts. Chellie, gripping the wet rock to steady herself, was aware that her nipples were hardening in involuntary response.

She was completely, almost voluptuously engrossed in the sheer physicality of the moment, yet some strange, almost animal instinct made her turn her head and glance over her shoulder.

Ash was standing on the other side of the pool, hands on hips and head slightly thrown back as he watched her. He looked casual, but the utter stillness of his stance betrayed him.

And she too was betrayed, her clothes lying in a pile at his feet. Unreachable.

For a few seconds she was frozen, her mind working feverishly. The temptation, of course, was to try to cover herself with her hands. But that was too much of a cliché, and besides, it sent out the signal that she wanted him to go on looking…

And I do, she thought. God help me, but I do.

There was only one other solution, and she took it swiftly and fiercely, jumping back into the pool, then treading water so that only her head and shoulders were visible.

'What the hell are you doing here?' She made her tone challenging.

'I invited myself to dinner,' he said. 'Rosalie's fish stew is renowned throughout the islands, and quite irresistible.' He paused. 'Like so much else at Arcadie.'

Chellie's mouth tightened. 'I mean why are you *here*? Now, and at this particular spot?'

He shrugged. 'Because this is my favourite place on the estate, and somehow I guessed you would find your way here too.' He smiled at her. 'It's a good place to be—isn't it?'

'Wonderful,' Chellie said crisply. 'But getting chilly now. So, I'd like to get out and get dressed. If you don't mind.'

'That's fine with me.' His voice was equable. 'But it can be a scramble when you're not used to it. You'd better take my hand.'

Chellie gasped. 'Like hell I will.'

'Do you have a choice?'

'Yes,' she said, trying to stop her teeth from chattering. 'I can stay here until you have the decency to go.'

'It's a little late to be prim, don't you think?' There was a ghost of laughter in his voice. 'Especially when the image of you standing under the cascade is now irrevocably etched into my brain.'

He paused for a moment, then began slowly to unbutton the white shirt he was wearing with immaculately pressed dark pants. 'Of course,' he said, 'I could always come in and join you. It's very hot today, and a little—stimulation might be pleasant.'

The breath caught in her throat. 'Don't you dare,' she said grittily. 'Don't you *bloody* dare.'

He laughed. 'You mean this pool isn't big enough for both of us? Well, you could be right. But you've also been in there quite long enough.'

He squatted down and held out his hand to her. 'Come on, take it before you get hypothermia,' he commanded. 'I'll even close my eyes if it will make you feel better,' he added caustically.

She swam a little closer. Warily. 'Then will you go—please?'

'No,' he said. 'But I will promise to turn my back.'

Which was like shutting the stable door when the horse was long gone, Chellie realised, fulminating.

She supposed that she could always stay where she was and brazen it out. Call his bluff. Except that she didn't feel very brazen. She felt cold, and shy, and hideously embarrassed. And not too far from tears either. Besides, Ash might not be bluffing.

Biting her lip hard, she swam to where he was waiting, eyes obediently closed. His fingers were warm and strong as they gripped hers, and she felt an unwelcome shock of pleasure at his touch.

She found a toehold under the water, and used it to push herself upwards, landing breathless and flurried on the rock beside him.

She said tautly, 'Thank you. Now turn your back, please.'

'As you wish.' He sounded as if he was grinning. 'May I say you looked much lovelier when you weren't blue with cold,' he added softly.

'Is that a fact?' Chellie said between her teeth, snatching up her clothes and holding them protectively against her. 'Well, you'll still be a bastard, no matter what colour you turn.'

'Tut, tut, Miss Greer,' Ash mocked. 'How very uptight you are. Anyone would think you'd never been skinny-dipping before.'

Chellie, desperately trying to force on her clothes over uncomfortably damp skin, didn't answer.

'That's it, isn't it?' he said slowly, after a pause. 'You never *have* done it—have you, Michelle? Another addition to the long list of experiences I suspect you've missed out on.'

'Then kindly keep your speculation to yourself,' Chellie flashed, dragging on her vest top and noting with alarm how revealingly it clung now, outlining her taut nipples in exquisite detail. 'My life is my own business.'

'You forget,' he said. 'As I told you before, I saved your life, which makes it mine now.'

'Well, I don't believe in ridiculous superstitions, and I belong to myself alone.'

'Alone?' Ash mused. 'Now, there's a chilly word.'

'How odd you should think so,' Chellie said coolly. 'Now, to me all it says is—independence.' She paused. 'And I'm dressed now.'

He turned back, scanning her, his eyes lingering unashamedly on the thrust of her breasts. 'So you are,' he said softly, his mouth twisting. 'But memory is a wonderful thing.'

'My vote goes to total amnesia,' she threw back at him. 'I'd give a lot to wipe out the events of the past few weeks—and especially the last forty-eight hours.'

His voice hardened. 'But unfortunately we're both stuck with them, Michelle, and there's no way out. So why don't we agree to make the best of things in the time we have left?' He paused. 'Rosalie and Cornelius believe we're friends, so I'd prefer to preserve the illusion.'

He held back the leaves of a tall shrub to enable her to pass.

'So, what do you think of Arcadie?' he added in a tone of polite enquiry.

'It's—amazing.' Chellie hesitated. 'This Mr Howard seems to have given you the total run of his house as well as his boat. You must be—lose.'

Ash shrugged. 'We've known each other a long time.'

And Julie? She thought the question, but did not dare ask it. Besides, didn't she already know the answer?

Hurriedly, she changed the subject. 'My passport,' she said. 'You forget to give it to me when we landed. Have you brought it with you?'

'Actually, no. It must still be on the boat. ' His sideways glance was faintly mocking. 'But don't worry. It's in a very safe place.'

'Yes,' Chellie said icily. 'I'm well aware of that.'

'I thought you would be,' he murmured. 'But full marks for trying.'

Chellie, trying in spite of everything to stalk ahead of him with dignity, nearly removed an eye on an intrusive branch.

When they finally reached the lawns, within sight of the house, she wheeled and faced him. 'Tell me something. We've established what you're doing here—you've come for Rosalie's fish stew. But what I don't understand is why

I should be stranded out in the wilds instead of staying in St Hilaire.'

'I'm sorry you feel stranded,' Ash said, after a pause. 'I arranged for you to be brought here because it's quiet and beautiful.'

'Yes, it is,' Chellie agreed. 'But it's also very isolated.'

'Surely that's part of its charm,' he returned. 'It's where I come when I need to chill out—do some thinking—get myself together for some reason. I hoped that was how it would appeal to you too.'

His voice dropped. 'And when I realised you'd found the pool I was convinced of it. Because for me that's the most magical place on the island.' His smile was wry. 'And from now on its enchantment will be doubled.'

Chellie bent her head, avoiding the intensity of his gaze, aware that her heart was fluttering like the wings of a trapped bird. She said, 'Don't—please…'

'Why not?' he asked quietly. 'Because at last I got to fulfil my fantasy? Because you were so lovely—and so vulnerable—that I would have walked across that water to reach you if you'd given me one sign? And because the image of every exquisite inch of you will haunt me for ever? Is that why you want me to keep silent?'

Colour stormed her face. She said in a stifled voice, 'You—must not say these things to me. You have no right…'

'No,' he said, and there was an odd note in his voice that sounded almost violent. 'You're quite correct, I don't. No right at all. But no amount of moral rectitude can stop me wishing. Just remember that.'

Chellie watched him stride away.

One sign, he'd said. *If you'd given me one sign.*

And only she would ever know how fatally close she'd come to doing exactly that. That she'd felt the force of his desire shiver like a warm, sweet wind over her naked body, and that for one brief, treacherous moment she'd gloried in it.

Fortunately she'd come to her senses in time, but every moment she spent in Ash's company represented real danger, and she had to be aware of that.

Her mouth twisted in a small, sad smile. 'But nothing can stop me wishing either,' she whispered, and made her way slowly back to the house.

In spite of the heat, Chellie felt cold and clammy when she reached her room. She stripped off her damp clothing and towelled herself down vigorously until her skin began to glow. She was just fastening the belt on the cream cotton robe that she'd found hanging in the closet when there was a knock on the bedroom door.

For a moment she tensed, wondering if it was Ash outside on the landing. Half-wishing for it to be so, but half-dreading it too. If she kept quiet, she thought, her visitor might deduce that she wasn't there and leave.

But there was a second, louder rap, and Rosalie's voice said, '*Mam'selle*, I have something for you.'

Chellie found herself sighing inwardly, and trailed over to open the door. Rosalie, smiling broadly, was holding a large flat box.

'This is yours, *mam'selle*. Mist' Ash says you left it behind.'

Chellie frowned in bewilderment. 'I think there's some mistake...'

Rosalie shook her head. 'It belongs to you, *mam'selle*. Mist' Ash said so.' Her voice was kind but firm.

'I think,' Chellie said, with a touch of grimness, 'I'd better have a word with Mist' Ash.'

'Oh, he's not here,' Rosalie informed her cheerfully. 'He had to go out, but he'll be back for dinner.' She gave a rich chuckle. 'He wouldn't miss my stew, that one.'

She planted the box into Chellie's reluctant hands and went off, humming a tune.

Chellie put the box down on the bed as if she was expecting it to explode. Everything she owned, and a lot that she didn't, was here with her, she thought, her frown deepening. She had no other possessions, and he knew it. So what was he playing at?

Gingerly, she raised the lid and parted the folds of tissue inside, catching her breath as she saw what was lying there. She lifted out the folds of grey silky fabric and held it against her. It was a dress, its mid-calf skirt cut on the bias, its bodice straight with narrow straps, and as she turned in front of the mirror she saw the faintly iridescent material change from pewter to silver with the movement.

The subtle colour enhanced the creaminess of her skin and the darkness of her hair. It was, she thought, exactly what she'd have chosen for herself.

A tiny voice in her head whispered, Try it on. But common sense told her to put it back in its box and never look at it again. Because she knew if she tried it that it would fit, and that she would not want to take it off again. And one of her main priorities must be to sever even the most fragile contact between Ash and herself.

She sighed, and began to re-fold the dress, her hands reluctant. As she did so, she noticed a slip of paper had fallen to the floor.

She retrieved it, and read the few hand-written words. It said simply:

Chellie, this is no big deal, so please don't throw it back at me.

And under his signature was a PS.

We could always pretend it's your birthday.

Chellie sank down on the edge of the bed and read the note over and over again until the words began to blur.

Where, she wondered bitterly, had Ash acquired this effortless ability to head her off at the pass?

Refusing to wear his gift now would only make her look at best ungracious, and at worst ridiculous, making a great fuss about nothing.

Except that it wasn't nothing, she thought with sudden anguish. In fact, it mattered far too much.

It occurred to her, without self-pity, that this was probably the first present a man had ever bought for her. And that included her father, whose gifts had always come via the nanny when she was little and his secretary when she was older.

Which made this all the more special, she thought with a stifled sigh, smoothing the fabric gently. And all the more taboo.

How could a man she hardly knew get something so completely right? she asked herself with a kind of desperation. Because in so many ways Ash was still a virtual stranger to her, and she must never forget that.

She might have been reticent, but she knew nothing about his own family—if he had one—or his background, which was clearly chequered. Maybe it was best to remain in ignorance, especially if he wasn't prepared to volunteer any information.

Their lives had touched—and that was all.

So why did their brief contact with each other seem infinitely more than that?

What made her feel that length of time, in itself, meant nothing? That in some strange way her whole life had been geared to meeting Ash, and that somehow it didn't matter that their acquaintance with each other could be measured in hours rather than years?

As soon as I saw him I knew, she thought with sudden helplessness. Knew that he was the one I'd always been waiting for. But why didn't Fate warn me that there could be no happy ending? That he was heavily involved with pretty blonde Julie, who probably has no shadows in her life or bitter mistakes to put right?

Why didn't my instincts tell me that, although my life

may belong to him, I never can? Because that's quite impossible, as he's made clear more than once.

He may be tempted, but he's also committed elsewhere. And he's not going to let a chance encounter spoil something good and real for him. A chance to leave the past behind him and establish himself, perhaps.

How could I have looked at him that night at Mama Rita's and not realised this? she wondered. Not seen that he was forbidden fruit? That he would always be prepared to step back out of the danger zone?

Because then, maybe, I could have saved myself a lifetime of heartache.

'"The joys of love",' she whispered sadly, wrapping her arms round her body, '"are but a moment long".'

But if I was offered that moment, she thought with sudden fierceness, I'd take it, and to hell with the consequences. I wouldn't make waves, or demand more than he was prepared to give. And at least I'd have something—some precious memory to take into the empty future.

Apart from this beautiful dress that she could not wear but which she would keep for ever.

She put the lid gently back on the box and tore up the note into infinitesimal pieces. Then she walked out on to the balcony and sat down on one of the cushioned loungers to watch the sunset. And to think.

She stayed in her room until the last possible moment. It was strange, but the black dress she'd brought from Mama Rita's no longer seemed quite so tacky, she thought, viewing herself in the full-length mirror. On the contrary, against the faint honey tan she'd acquired it looked cool and sexy.

But would that be enough? Would *she* be enough?

Well, she thought, straightening her shoulders. This was her chance to find out.

Ash was in the sitting room, standing by the long glazed doors leading to the verandah, staring into the darkness, drink in hand.

As Chellie came hesitantly into the room he turned to look at her, his brows lifting as he scanned the uncovered shoulders and the long, slim tanned legs revealed by the brief skirt. There was a slow and tingling silence. Then he raised his glass, the blue eyes hooded, his mouth smiling faintly. He said softly, 'Not your birthday, after all. But mine, perhaps.' The words lingered tantalisingly in the air.

Chellie shrugged. 'I decided to stick to familiar territory.'

'Very brave,' he said. 'In view of the memories it must revive.'

She lifted her chin, meeting his gaze squarely. 'Oh, they weren't all bad.' She paused. 'But the dress you sent me was spectacular,' she added with assumed nonchalance. 'For someone who sails other people's boats for a living, you clearly know a lot about women's clothes.'

'There's probably a cheap crack just waiting to be made,' Ash drawled. 'But I'll pass.'

'Very wise,' she said. 'And I'm sure you'll find some other lucky lady to benefit from your good taste.'

'I bought it for you.' His mouth tightened. 'It can't have been pleasant—having to wear someone else's clothes all the time on top of everything else that's happened recently. Just for once, I wanted you to have something that was all your own.'

Pain twisted inside her. She thought, *And I want that too—so badly.*

Aloud, she said stiltedly, 'Well—that's—a very kind thought.'

Or is it? she wondered. Could it be that he just doesn't like seeing me in his lady's clothes? That was another distinct possibility and it stung her to the core.

'And here's another thought, even kinder.' He walked to a side-table and picked up a jug. 'Let me introduce you to Planter's Punch—Cornelius-style. It's well worth trying— but strictly in moderation,' he added, pouring some of the liquid into a tumbler and adding ice, sliced lemon and a sprig of mint.

Chellie took a cautious sip, and blenched. 'Hell's bells—what's in it?'

'Apart from local rum, I haven't the vaguest idea.' Ash shrugged. 'Corney plays his cards close to his chest.'

'Corney?' She forced a smile. 'He seems far too dignified for nicknames.'

'Perhaps,' he said. 'But he forgives me a great deal.'

She took another sip, sending him a glinting look from beneath her lashes. 'I wonder what range of sins that covers?'

'Better,' he said, 'not to go there, I think. Although you'd probably be disappointed.'

She ran the tip of her tongue round her lips. 'You're saying that Cornelius has never had a serious strain placed on his loyalty? You amaze me.'

'I didn't think,' he said, 'that I was saying very much at all.'

'No,' she mused. 'You're very restrained. Or do I mean constrained? I'm not really sure.'

'Put that down,' he said, 'to the Planter's Punch. It attacks the brain cells and destroys rational thought, not to mention behaviour. Let me save you from yourself.' He took the glass from her hand and placed it on a nearby table. 'And now I think it's time we were going into dinner.'

Chellie hung back. She said in a low voice, 'Perhaps I don't want to be saved. Has that occurred to you?'

Ash paused, looking down at her, his expression wry. He said, 'A lot of things have occurred to me, and when we've eaten you and I need to have a serious talk. Now, come on, before Rosalie gets cross.'

It seemed, Chellie thought as, subdued, she followed him across the hall to a low-ceilinged dining room, its long table gleaming with silver and crystal, that she'd gambled and lost on the first throw.

But, in spite of everything, the delicious meal that followed was bound to lift her spirits to some extent. They began with a chilled avocado soup, followed by the hot and spicy fish stew, served with sweet potatoes and a green vegetable that she didn't recognise, but which, Ash told her, was called callaloo. Accompanying this was a pale, dry white wine, crisp and clear on the palate to offset the rich food. To finish, there were mango sorbets, and a wonderful creamy pudding tasting of coconut.

Ash kept the conversation general, chatting mainly about the island's history and its plans for the future, the modest expansion of tourism, making her relax and respond in spite of herself.

But then he was bound to keep off personal topics, she realised, in deference to the presence of Cornelius, who was waiting at table.

Acting as chaperon, perhaps? she thought drily. Looking out for the interests of the owner's daughter.

But when the meal was over, and coffee and brandies were served, she was surprised to hear Cornelius wishing them goodnight.

'Thanks, Corney.' Ash sent him a swift smile. 'And tell Rosalie that her fish stew still has no rivals.'

Cornelius acknowledged the compliment with a benign nod, and withdrew.

'And now,' Ash said quietly, 'we have things to discuss.' He paused, reaching into his back pocket and producing her passport, which he pushed across the candlelit table. 'I got you this.'

'Oh.' For a moment she was completely taken aback. 'Well—thank you.' She picked it up. 'Did you make a special trip to St Hilaire before dinner to collect it?'

Ash shrugged. 'It seemed to be an issue. It was time to resolve it.'

Chellie smiled extra-brightly. 'In time to prove my identity to the consul on Monday?'

'If you want to wait till then.' He was leaning back in his chair and she could not see his expression.

She said, 'I don't understand. What alternative do I

have?' And felt her heart begin to thud in excitement as she wondered what he was going to say.

'If I lent you some money you could be out of here tomorrow,' he said abruptly. 'You could take a local plane to Barbados or Grenada, and branch off from there to anywhere you wanted.'

There was a silence. Her hands were trembling, and she clasped them together tightly in her lap under the shelter of the table.

'Why would I wish to do that?'

'Because, as you've said, you need to get on with your life. This could help you on your way.'

'It's good of you,' she said slowly. 'But I think you've done enough. I'm a British citizen in trouble, and the consul is obliged to help me.'

'So, what are you going to tell him?' Ash asked laconically. 'Are you going to spill the beans about Ramon and Mama Rita's?' He shook his head. 'I don't think he'll be too impressed. Whereas I already know about your various misfortunes. Think about it. Sleep on it, and I'll come back for your answer in the morning.'

'You're not staying here tonight?' The question was too quick, too urgent, and Chellie felt her face warm.

There was a brief pause, then, 'I decided against it,' he said.

'I see.' Chellie pushed back her chair and rose. 'Please don't let me detain you.'

The sitting room was lit with shaded lamps when she marched in, her head held high, and unexpectedly there was music, with a slow, sensuous, unfamiliar rhythm, playing softly from a concealed system.

'You left your brandy.' Ash had followed her.

'I probably shouldn't have any more alcohol,' she told him curtly. 'Or I might say and do something I could regret.'

He sighed. 'Chellie, I've approached all this in the wrong way. Made a complete mess of it.'

'On the contrary,' she said. 'Everything's crystal-clear.

You need to get on with your own life too, and you can't do that while you still feel responsible for me. So it would be convenient if I was out of the way.' She gave a taut smile. 'So maybe I'll take you up on your offer, after all.'

'Understand this,' Ash said. 'I am not trying to get rid of you. At least, not in the way you think.'

'How many ways are there?' she demanded raggedly. 'Not that it matters. Because I don't have to sleep on it. I'll take your kind offer, and be out of here tomorrow.' She paused. 'And I'll pay you back every single cent,' she added fiercely. 'No matter how long it takes.'

'In that case,' he said, apparently unmoved by her vehemence, let's drink a toast—to the future.'

Chellie shrugged and lifted her glass. 'To the future,' she echoed, and drank defiantly.

But inside her there was pain. In a few moments he would be leaving for St Hilaire, and tomorrow her last sight of him would probably be from the window of some plane.

Why was he making her leave like this? Had he suddenly heard that his girlfriend was arriving, and didn't relish having to explain Chellie's presence in her home?

If that was the case, she had very little time left.

Oh, please, she appealed silently to the listening Fates. Let me have my single moment—my one night—and I'll take the heartbreak when it comes.

Aloud, she said, 'Is it wise to drink if you intend to drive?'

'Obviously not,' he said. 'But Corney will take me, if I ask him.'

'Yes,' she said. 'Of course. How silly of me.' She paused again. 'Tell me something—what is this music? I don't recognise it.'

'It's the *beguine*,' Ash told her. 'We have Rosalie to thank for it. She was born on Martinique, and sometimes her origins come roaring back.' He grimaced. 'Like tonight.'

'Well, I'm with Rosalie,' Chellie said. 'It's beautiful.'

She began to move slowly round the room in time with

the beat, giving herself over completely to the haunting rhythm, swaying her hips gently as she danced, allowing her natural grace full rein, without inhibition.

She did not need to glance over her shoulder to know that Ash was watching her, his eyes locked on her as if mesmerised.

Perhaps, she thought, her heart beginning to bump, the night was not over yet, after all. Perhaps…

His voice reached her softly, but urgently. 'Chellie—whatever you're doing, stop it.'

'Why?' She let the brief black skirt swirl enticingly as she swung round to face him, to challenge him, her emerald-dark eyes heavy with desire. 'You wanted this once—you wanted me to dance for you. So—why not now?'

'For all kinds of reasons,' he said almost grimly. He walked over to her and took her hand, pulling her towards him so that she was in his arms, but not touching. He held her firmly, moving with her in perfect cohesion.

'Dance with me, Chellie,' he directed quietly. 'Not for me. It's safer that way.'

'Why does it always have to be safe?' she demanded huskily. 'You come close, and then you back away. Why is that?'

'Because I always remember, just in time, I have no right to be that near.' His tone roughened. 'Because there are things about me—about this whole situation—that you need to know. Things that we have to talk about because they could change everything.'

'No,' she said, her voice shaking. 'You don't have to tell me—anything. It isn't necessary. Because I already know what you're trying to say.'

'You *know*?' He halted, staring at her. 'Was it Laurent?' he asked sharply. 'Did he say something?'

'No, nothing like that.' Chellie hunched a shoulder. 'He—he was very discreet. I—just guessed. I—I'm not a complete fool.'

'Oh, dear God.' His voice was almost blank. 'You have to let me explain…'

'No.' She spoke on a note of desperation. 'I know—and that's enough. I don't want everything spelled out for me, Ash. Spare me that, please.'

He said heavily, 'If that's what you want.' He hesitated. 'I didn't intend any of this, Chellie—not for a moment. You have to believe that. And I should never have allowed it to happen.'

'And there's something you should know too.' She looked up at him, her eyes pleading as they met his. 'I—don't care.'

He sighed. 'Then maybe you should.'

'Even if I swear that it will make no difference—that I'll leave as planned?' Her fingers bit into his arms through the thin shirt. 'Ash, I promise you I won't be a nuisance. Whatever happens between us will be our secret always, and I'll never pressure you in any way. Or ask you for anything you can't give.' She swallowed. 'You must believe that. No one will suffer because of this.'

'You don't think so?' His crooked smile held bitterness. 'I wish I could be so sure.'

'Unless you don't want me,' she said. Her voice trembled. 'Is that the real truth, Ash? Is it that simple.'

'Oh, I want you,' he said. 'And have done from the moment I first saw you. On the damned boat I hardly had an hour's sleep, and I was fighting all the time to keep my hands off you.'

'Then don't go tonight,' she whispered. 'Stay here. Stay with me—please.'

'Wild horses,' he said softly, 'could not drag me away.'

And he lifted her into his arms and carried her out of the room, through the shadowed hallway to the stairs beyond.

CHAPTER NINE

IIN HER bedroom, the lamp on the night table had been lit and the cover on the bed turned down.

Ash put Chellie gently on her feet. He framed her face in his hands, looking deep into her eyes, his smile faintly troubled.

'You're trembling,' he told her quietly. 'What is there to frighten you?'

I wish my hair hadn't been hacked off. I wish I wasn't feeling so awkward and inexperienced. And, most of all, I wish I was beautiful, with blonde hair and perfect teeth.

'Only myself,' she said. 'I'm scared of disappointing you.'

A faint laugh shook him. He drew her close, resting his lips against her hair. 'Now, how could you possibly do that?'

'Because it's happened before.' Her voice was a thread. 'He said I—I didn't know what to do to satisfy a man. That I was useless—not a real woman.'

'Dear God,' he said bleakly. 'But you must surely have known it wasn't true? Or were your previous experiences equally disastrous?'

She shook her head. 'I didn't have any. Ramon was the first. The only way I can judge myself.'

There was a silence, then he said quietly, 'I'm sorry, Chellie. I didn't know. I thought...' He paused again. 'Oh, to hell with what I thought.'

She closed her eyes, breathing the warm, clean scent of him. 'You said you'd had this fantasy about me, which you'd now fulfilled.' She tried to smile. 'Maybe we should keep it like that and I should quit while I'm ahead.'

'Firstly,' Ash said, very gently, 'do not—ever—confuse me with Ramon again. Secondly, and more importantly, my original fantasy has changed a little since this afternoon. You're still exquisitely naked, but now you're in bed with me, in my arms, and I can touch as well as look. And I dream that you're kissing me—that your body's opening to me. That you're taking me into you so deeply it's almost an agony. And that you're sighing my name as you come.'

'Oh, God,' she said. She was still trembling, but now it was with a longing she had no need to disguise. She could feel the heat rising in her veins, bring a soft, awakened flush to her skin.

She put her arms round his neck, drawing him down to her. Just before his lips met hers, she whispered, 'You dream the most wonderful things.'

'And now we'll make them come true,' he said. 'Together.'

His mouth was warm as it caressed hers, and tender too, his passion carefully held in check. Waiting, she knew, for her.

She responded ardently, her lips parting beneath his, longing for the kiss to deepen, to offer the intimacy she longed for.

She was not disappointed. At once his arms tightened round her, and she felt the hot invasion of his tongue exploring the inner sweetness of her mouth.

When he raised his head the blue eyes were drowsy, clouded with desire. His fingers skimmed her bare shoulders, lingering on each plane and curve as if sculpting her image, then moving down to the first swell of her breasts above the bodice, gently smoothing the warm flesh.

She turned her head, pressing her cheek to his hand with a small, choked murmur of pleasure and need.

His hand moved, found the zip at the side of the dress, and began to release it, letting the bodice peel away from her naked breasts.

His lips found her ear, teasing the lobe with his teeth,

then moving down to plant soft kisses down the vulnerable curve of her throat.

'Just looking will never be enough again,' he whispered. 'I want all of you.'

Her breasts seemed to bloom as his hands stroked them, her nipples hardening in sheer delight under the tender, sensuous play of his fingertips. He cupped them gently, bending to adore them with his mouth, his tongue flickering on the sensitised peaks.

He undid the zip completely, allowing the dress to drift down and pool round her feet, leaving her in nothing but the minuscule G-string. She heard him catch his breath, then felt his hands moving on her in gentle, tantalising exploration, moulding the curve of her hips and the smooth softness of her thighs. Creating a slow, languid torment which ached deep within her.

She murmured something incoherent—pleading—pressing her burning forehead against his chest.

Ash slid down her last tiny covering, then lifted her from the tangle of clothing at her feet and placed her on the bed. He lay down beside her, drawing her close to him, finding her mouth with his.

When she could speak, she whispered, 'You haven't taken your clothes off.'

'There's plenty of time for that,' he returned softly. 'We have the whole night ahead of us—and this part of it's for you.'

He began to caress her again, his mouth following the passage of his unhurried hands down her body, finding every pulse, each soft, secret place. When, finally, he reached the parting of her thighs, his touch was as light as gossamer on her yielding womanhood, the cool, clever fingers creating an alchemy all their own as they stroked the tiny sheltered bud.

Chellie could hear the huskiness of her own breathing, the quickening throb of her heart as her body responded helplessly, adoringly, to the delicate intensity of pleasure that he was building for her.

Her body was writhing in a fever of excitement as he brought her again and again to the brink of the unknown, his lips on her breasts, tugging sweetly at her aroused nipples, circling them with his tongue, then moving back to her mouth, biting sensuously at her lower lip.

The spiral of sensation mounting inside her was suddenly too wild—too consuming—and in some far reeling corner of her mind she understood that this was complete and utter surrender. That she could faint—that she might die—but she would never be able to—stop—because it was—too late, and all control was gone.

And as she reached the ultimate, glittering peak, and pleasure took her like a sea wave, tossing her in endless billows of rapture, she felt tears on her face and heard herself moaning his name.

She lay spent and breathless in his arms, while he kissed her wet eyes and her parted lips, murmuring to her how lovely she was, and how clever. Calling her his darling and his sweet, passionate angel.

When she was capable of speech, she said, gasping, 'So—that's how it's supposed to be.'

Ash kissed her again. 'Only for the lucky people.'

'All the same.' Chellie slid a hand inside his shirt, stroking his warm chest, coaxing the flat male nipples into erection. 'Wasn't it rather—one-sided?'

There was a smile in his voice. 'Just a little, perhaps. But that was quite intentional.'

'Why?'

'Because I needed to prove something to you.'

'Which is?'

He said gently, 'That you could never be a disappointment, sexually or in any other way. Because you, Chellie Greer, are all woman.'

'That,' she said, 'is quite the nicest thing anyone ever said to me.'

'You're welcome,' Ash said gravely. 'And please don't stop what you're doing,' he added lazily. 'I like it.'

She began undoing his shirt. 'But you're going to enjoy this far more,' she murmured. 'You see, I have a few little fantasies of my own to indulge.'

'Oh,' he said. 'And undressing me is one of them?'

'It's a beginning, anyway.'

'I see,' Ash said thoughtfully. 'You're not planning any real recovery time, then? Or even a breathing space?'

She slipped his shirt off and tossed it to the floor. 'You said I was all woman. I have to live up to my reputation.' Her fingers strayed downward to the zip of his pants and tugged experimentally.

He said a little hoarsely, 'So far, it's doing fine.'

'You've seen nothing yet.' She eased the pants down over his hips, and discarded them too.

'I only hope I survive.' His voice was uneven.

'I don't think you're in much danger.' She pretended to consider. 'After all, this may be my first time, but it certainly isn't yours.'

His hands closed on hers, halting them, the blue eyes suddenly serious as they met hers. 'Chellie—I think we should let the past take care of itself. A month—two months ago I didn't even know you existed.'

She bent forward and kissed him on the mouth, running the tip of her tongue across his lips. She said, 'But you know now, don't you?'

'Yes.' In one swift movement, Ash stripped off his briefs and turned on to his back, lifting her over him. And with a soft groan of satisfaction he lowered her slowly on to him.

Chellie stared down at him, eyes widening as she experienced the full heated strength of him inside her at last. As she felt her body close round him and possess him.

Ash looked back at her, his grin wicked, sensuous. He said, 'Well?'

'Yes,' she said, her breath catching in her throat. 'Oh,

yes...' And she began to move, tentatively at first, but then gaining in confidence under his husky encouragement.

He watched her through half-closed eyes as his hands ranged over her, worshipping every slender curve, enticing every nerve-ending into glowing life. He stroked down her back, from her shoulders to her flanks, and she shivered with delight, her spine arching fiercely in response, her round breasts engorged and throbbing.

Their joined bodies rose and sank in complete attunement, in mutual demand.

She could feel the inner tension building in her again. Found herself at once overtaken—pierced by a pleasure so strong it was almost anguish—and sent, her whole body shaking and quivering, into the glory of release. She cried out sharply, in a kind of disbelief that heaven could be there for her once more so soon, and Ash answered her, groaning in ecstasy as his body shuddered into its own climax.

Afterwards, they lay very quietly together, his arms wrapped round her, her head tucked into his shoulder.

He whispered, 'Are you all right.'

'I think,' she said, 'that I'm in a thousand little pieces.'

'Is that all?' He kissed the top of her head very tenderly. 'I'll have to try and do better.'

She realised that she wanted very badly to tell him that she loved him. But that was impossible. It would go completely against the set of rules she had imposed on herself. And, if nothing else, pride should keep her silent. Because, very soon now, she would be walking away from him for ever, and she needed to be able to do it with her head held high. No embarrassing declarations to muddy the waters.

'Is something wrong?' he asked.

She swallowed. 'Not a thing. Why do you ask?'

He said slowly, 'Because one moment you were totally relaxed, like a sleeping baby. The next—not.'

'Imagination can play strange tricks.' She stroked his cheek. 'But perhaps I really do need to sleep for a while.'

'Only for a while?' He captured her hand and kissed its palm. She could feel his smile against her skin.

'Certainly,' she said. 'I don't want to miss anything.'

Ash reached out an arm and switched off the lamp. 'I promise,' he said solemnly, 'not to start without you.'

He slept almost at once, but Chellie could not. She lay in his embrace, not wishing to move in case she disturbed him, and stared into the darkness.

There, in the shadows, was her future, she thought. Without light, and without hope. And she felt frightened, and more alone than she had ever been in her life before.

She dozed eventually, only to be woken by his mouth planting a trail of gentle kisses down her body. She turned to him, her mouth eager, her hands caressing him with total candour. This time their lovemaking was slow, and almost achingly tender.

As if, she thought, their bodies were saying goodbye. Which was no more than the truth.

They did not speak any words. There was instead the intimacy of sighs and murmurs, and infinitesimal changes of breathing to chart their passage to rapture. And when the moment of culmination came, Ash wrapped her close in his arms and held her as if he would never let her go.

Ah, but he will, Chellie thought sadly. He will.

The pain of love, it seemed, had already begun. And when sleep finally claimed her she was glad.

'Miss Greer—*mam'selle*. I have coffee for you.'

Chellie opened unwilling eyes to find the room bathed in sunlight and Rosalie standing by the bed, cup and saucer in hand. In the same instant she registered that she was alone.

The bed beside her was empty, the pillows plumped, the sheet smooth as glass. No sign at all that anyone had shared it with her. No untidy muddle of clothing on the floor. No sound of running water from the shower either.

Ash had gone, and all traces of the night they'd spent together had been removed.

Expertly removed, Chellie thought with sudden bitterness. But why was she surprised? After all, if you were sleeping with the daughter of the house it was bad policy to enjoy another girl in her absence, especially when loyal family retainers were involved.

Ash clearly knew how to cover his tracks—maybe not for the first time.

And if some secret corner of her heart had hoped for a miracle—had prayed that the splendour of passion they had shared might lead to some kind of commitment on his part—then she knew better now.

She sat up slowly, holding the covering sheet to her breasts. 'Thank you, Rosalie.'

'And Mr Ash called. He has a seat for you on the noon flight to Grenada.'

Chellie nearly spilled her coffee all over the bed. 'He called?' she repeated incredulously. 'When?'

'Half an hour ago, *mam'selle*. He also say a car will be sent for you at eleven.'

'I see.' Her mouth was dry. 'Was—was there any other message?' she managed.

'No, *mam'selle*,' Rosalie assured her cheerfully. 'Shall I run your bath?'

'No—no, thank you.' Chellie forced a smile. 'I can manage.'

So, she thought drearily when she was alone. Last night was then, this is now, and what worlds apart they are.

But then what had she expected? She'd appealed to him on a strictly sexual level and he'd taken her. That had been the deal, and it was much too late for regrets.

She stretched, feeling the voluptuous ache in her body, the singing of her pulses. She might be on the floor emotionally, but physically she felt wonderful.

Ash had taught her to be a woman, she thought, and she would always be grateful to him for that. But she had also learned to feel with a woman's heart, and she would never be free again.

She didn't want the coffee, but she needed the boost of caffeine it offered to clear her head and get her moving. After all, she had packing to do. It was time for her, too, to pretend she had never been here.

As promised, Rosalie had washed and pressed the linen dress, and it was hanging on the wardrobe door. But she wasn't going to wear it, or anything else that belonged to Julie. The thought was unbearable.

She would make do with the handful of her own stuff that she'd brought, and buy herself a change of underwear on Grenada for the journey home. Everything else could stay behind.

Except for the dress Ash had bought her, she thought with a pang. She would take that with her—as a salutary reminder of the gulf that existed between sex and love. And a warning never to allow herself to confuse them again.

I don't want to wake up and find the bed beside me empty ever again, she thought, as she pushed back the sheet and swung her legs to the floor. And if that means spending the rest of my life alone, so be it. I've been alone before.

Brave words, but she knew that it would never be as easy as that. Because it would not just be a dress that she would take with her. Ash would go too—the sound of his voice, the unique male scent of him, the taste of his mouth and the controlled drive of his body, taking her to rapture and beyond.

Potent memories, she thought, and also completely inescapable. Something she would have to learn to live with.

She showered, and dressed in her denim skirt and tee shirt. Full circle, she thought, as she set about re-packing her bag.

There was pitifully little to go in it, she mused, frowningly, and then realised why. The black dress she'd worn last night was unaccountably missing.

She hunted through the wardrobe, and even searched under the bed, but there was no sign of it.

Oh, hell, she thought, biting her lip. Rosalie's probably

pounced on it for laundering. What on earth will she make of the G-string? At least I won't be around to find out, she added with a mental shrug.

The last remaining item was the precious passport, which was still downstairs on the sitting room table.

She picked up her bag, gave the room a last, lingering look, then went downstairs.

Rosalie met her in the hall. 'Mr Ash is here,' she announced, sending Chellie's heart into painful free-fall. 'Out on the verandah. I'm making him scrambled eggs. You want some too?'

'No—no, thanks. I'm not hungry.'

Rosalie sent her a disparaging glance. 'You're too thin, *mam'selle*. Should eat more.'

'Ah.' Chellie tried to keep her voice light. 'Someone once said you could never be too rich or too thin. One out of two isn't bad.'

Rosalie snorted and went back to the kitchen, leaving Chellie to make her reluctant way into the sitting room. If she hadn't needed to collect her passport she'd have been tempted to bolt back upstairs again. Even so, if she was quick and quiet…

'Good morning.' The verandah doors were wide open and he was standing there, dark against the brilliance of the sunlight.

Her hopes of evasion dashed, Chellie lifted her chin, trying to ignore the jolt to her senses. 'Oh, hi.' She attempted a casual note. 'I got your message. I wasn't expecting to see you.'

'I wasn't expecting to be here,' he returned. 'But there's been a change of plan. I've found out there's an earlier plane. If we leave straight after breakfast, you can catch it.'

She picked up her passport and stowed it in her bag, aware that her hands were trembling.

'I see.' She forced a smile. 'You—you really can't wait to be rid of me, can you?'

'I've booked you a room at the Oceanside Club,' he went

on, as if she hadn't spoken. 'And I'll join you there as soon as I can. There are issues here that I have to deal with first.'

'Issues?' Chellie repeated slowly. She had a sudden graphic image of Julie, with her bright smile dimmed, her eyes blurred with tears. 'Is that how you describe hurting people—messing with their emotions?'

His brows lifted. 'I wasn't aware that there was much emotion involved,' he said drily. 'But I'm prepared to stand corrected.' He paused. 'Whatever—I think it's better if you're away from here while I sort things out,' he added levelly. 'You'll just have to trust me on this.'

'Ash,' she said. 'We can't do this. We agreed that last night was all there could ever be, and nothing's changed.'

'You don't think so?' He shook his head. 'You're wrong, Chellie. Last night only proved what I've always known— that we belong together.' He came further into the room. 'Darling, I won't let you go.' His voice deepened. 'I can't. And I'll do whatever it takes to give us the freedom to be together.' He came to her, taking her hands in his. 'I thought you'd want that too? Am I wrong?'

'No.' Chellie's voice was wretched. 'I do want it. Oh, so much. But I know that you can't build happiness on the ruins of someone else's life.'

He stared at her. 'Chellie—you can't honestly believe that applies to us.'

She looked down at the floor. 'I think it could.' She jumped as the front doorbell pealed imperatively. 'I—I suppose that's my lift to the airport.'

Ash frowned. 'No, I'm your lift. And I wasn't expecting visitors,' he added with a touch of grimness as Cornelius went past the sitting room to answer the door. 'At least, not yet.'

'I'm here to see Miss Greer.' A man's voice, loud and slightly hectoring, filled the hall. 'Take me to her, please.'

Chellie's lips parted in a gasp of shock. 'My God,' she breathed. 'It's Jeffrey—Jeffrey Chilham. But how can it be? It's impossible.'

Cornelius was murmuring something in reply, but the caller responded with a snort.

'That's nonsense, my good man. I know quite well she's here. And that Brennan fellow too, I've no doubt. Kindly let me pass.'

Ash's hands gripped hers more tightly. 'Who the hell is this?' His voice was urgent.

Chellie shook her head helplessly. 'He works for my father.'

'Dear God.' Ash's mouth tightened harshly. 'So he couldn't even come in person.'

She stared at him. 'What are you talking about?'

He said wearily, 'I think you're about to find out.'

The next minute, Jeffrey Chilham was filling the doorway. He was a tall man, with greying hair and a red face that heat and irritation had rendered brick-coloured.

The khaki shorts he was wearing with a multi-coloured shirt did him no favours at all, and he was fanning himself vigorously with a Panama hat.

'Michelle,' he exclaimed. 'My dear girl. Thank heavens you're safe.' He stared at her, his lips pursed in disapproval. 'But your hair looks terrible. What have you done to it?'

'It was cut.' Chellie faced him unsmilingly. 'Jeffrey, what are you doing here?'

'My dear, do you really need to ask?' His chest swelled importantly. 'I've come to take you home, of course. Although I don't recommend presenting yourself to your father looking as you do,' he added, frowning. 'Perhaps while your hair is growing again you should wear a wig.'

'I did,' she said. 'It didn't suit me.' She realised that she suddenly felt cold. She was still gripping Ash's hand, and quietly detached herself. 'And how exactly did you know how to find me?'

'Well, naturally we have Brennan here to thank for that.' He gave Ash a condescending nod. 'Sir Clive is naturally grateful for your efforts in rescuing Miss Greer, my man, but he is not pleased that you ignored his explicit instructions to bring her back to England. Sending me halfway across the world has cost him time and money, and he has informed your company that he intends to negotiate a reduction in your fee as a result.'

His words fell into a silence that was as deep as an ocean.

Chellie found herself suddenly struggling for breath. When she could move, she swung round and stared at Ash, who was standing stony-faced, his arms folded across his chest.

'Is it true?' she asked huskily. 'What he's saying? Did you know who I was all along?'

'Yes,' he said. 'I knew.' His voice was expressionless. 'You'd been tracked to Santo Martino by other operatives, then the trail went cold and I came to find you myself.'

'Paid—by my father?' The muscles in her throat were taut with pain and she felt physically sick. 'He—hired you?'

Jeffrey Chilham laughed. 'Of course, my dear. Mr Brennan and his partner are businessmen. They run a specialist security organisation. Personal protection, tracing missing persons, negotiating over hostages—that kind of thing. 'Mr Brennan signed a highly-paid contract with us. Or did you think he did it for love?'

'No,' Chellie said quietly. 'I never thought that.' She wrapped her arms round her body, trying to control the violent internal shivering assailing her. She turned back to Ash, still standing rigidly beside her. 'Well, no one can say that you don't earn your money,' she added with icy scorn. 'Does everyone get your particular brand of personal service—or is there an extra charge?'

Ash winced, his mouth tightening. He said, 'Chellie— listen to me. I was going to tell you. To explain. I swear it. I thought—I hoped we'd have more time.'

'We had time on the boat,' she said. 'How long does it take to tell me I've been sold out?'

'It wasn't that simple,' he said. 'Not at first. Because I believed you were just another assignment, and a tricky one at that. 'And I'd been enjoined to secrecy by your father. It was part of the deal. He claimed that you were stubborn, and wilful, and might refuse to go with me or even run away again if you knew the truth.'

Chellie drew an angry, shaking breath. 'Well, he was right about that.'

'But I realised almost at once that you didn't want to be returned to him,' Ash went on. 'You barely mentioned him, so it was clear there was no love lost between you. Everything you said was about making a new life for yourself—finding some kind of independence. And I could understand why. I only met your father once, and it seemed even then that he was more angry than anxious about you. He spoke about you as if you were a parcel that had gone astray.'

He paused. 'He also implied that this wasn't the first time you'd got into a mess. That you were some wild child who'd never done a day's work in her life and slept her way round London, but that Ramon was a scandal too far and he wanted it dealt with quietly and confidentially.'

Chellie caught her breath. 'Oh, God. And you—believed him?'

'He was paying me to find you, Chellie, not to make moral judgements. And I'd seen the newspaper file on you. It seemed to confirm his story.'

He threw his head back. 'But then I met you,' he added flatly. 'And I began to wonder. Because you were a million miles from the cold-hearted, extravagant little tart that he'd described. You were brave and vulnerable, sexy and scared all at the same time. And so innocent you almost broke my heart.

'So that's why I refused to take you to London. I wanted to see your father out of his usual territory—watch how he behaved towards you and then take the appropriate action.' He shook his head. 'I still can't believe he hasn't come in person.'

'Sir Clive is a very busy man,' Jeffrey Chilham put in, his voice shocked. 'And it isn't as if Michelle has been hurt in any way—or locked up and held to ransom. Naturally, under those circumstances, he would have rushed to her side.' He looked uncomfortable. 'But there's been no real harm done. She—she just made an unfortunate choice of man, that's all.'

'I seem to make a habit of it,' Chellie said bitterly. She turned back to Ash. 'So why were you trying to hustle me off to Grenada? Did you plan to hide me so that you could extort some more money from my loving father?' She paused. 'I wonder what my actual market value is? I'll have to remember to ask him.'

Ash moved quickly, almost violently, and took her by the shoulders. 'You know that isn't true.' His voice was low and tense. The blue eyes burned into hers. 'I wasn't going to hand you back against your will to someone who didn't care about you. That's the truth. You must believe me.'

'Why should I?' Chellie lifted her chin defiantly. 'When you've lied to me from the first moment I saw you.' Her derisive laugh cracked in the middle. '*Someone to watch over me?* God, what a joke.'

She shook her head. 'And I made it so easy for you, didn't I—the rich man's stupid daughter? You provided the bait, and I practically dragged you into bed. Why, Ash? Did you decide that your present girlfriend's father had less to offer than mine?'

'What the hell are you talking about?' Ash said roughly. 'I have no girlfriend.' His mouth twisted as he looked down at her. 'Although I did think I had a lover.'

'No,' she said. 'You had a dupe. A blind, trusting dupe. But my eyes are open now, so you'd better revert to Plan A and go on courting the owner's daughter. I hope she finds out what you're really like before the walk down the aisle.'

'The owner's daughter?' His voice sparked with incredulity. 'Are you crazy?'

'I was,' she said. 'But not any more. And please take your hands off me.'

'Michelle!' Jeffrey Chilham's voice was sharp. 'I'm trying to be patient here, but do I infer that you've had some kind of relationship with this man?'

'No,' she said. 'No relationship. He took me to bed last night, that's all. I suppose he viewed it as an unofficial bonus.'

Ash released her and took a step back. He said courteously, 'No, I thought it was a foretaste of heaven.'

He took a deep breath. 'Chellie, my love, you have to listen to me, please. Because you've got things so terribly wrong.' His voice was gentle, almost pleading. 'You have every right to be angry, but I never meant you to find out like this. I thought Grenada would give us a breathing space. Give me time to explain properly.'

'Explain? Or invent another tissue of lies? Thank God I was spared that, at least,' she added with contempt.

'No,' he said. 'So that I could tell you everything and we could start again, with no secrets—all our cards on the table.'

She said slowly, 'Do you know—if this wasn't so hideous, it would almost be funny? But I'm not in the mood for jokes.'

She looked at Jeffrey Chilham, who was standing, his face mottled with shock and anger.

She said, 'I presume that all the arrangements to get me back to the UK have been made with my father's usual efficiency? Then I may as well take advantage of them. Let's go.'

'Very well,' he said stiffly. 'Although you realise I shall have to make a full report to Sir Clive.' He cast a fulminating look at Ash. 'And you'd better start looking for another job—if you can find one. You've made a bad enemy today, my friend.'

'That,' Ash said curtly, 'is the least of my problems.'

He turned on his heel and walked out into the garden.

Chellie watched him go. The numbness of betrayal was beginning to wear off, and she wanted to sink to her knees and howl her loss and loneliness to the smiling sky.

But I can't cry, she told herself with icy determination. Not yet. Because I have to go back, and somehow restart my life.'

A life, she thought, as pain twisted inside her, without love. And which would take every scrap of courage she possessed.

CHAPTER TEN

'DISGUSTING,' Jeffrey said in a furious undertone, his voice shaking. 'Disgraceful. I am lost for words to describe your behaviour.'

'Really?' Chellie sent him a frozen smile. 'I would never have guessed.'

The ride to St Hilaire's small airport had been an uncomfortable one. Chellie, racked by her own unhappy thoughts and still stunned by Ash's betrayal, had hardly exchanged two words with Jeffrey, glum and brooding beside her.

But it had been too good to last. Almost as soon as their private aircraft was airborne, on its way to Barbados, Jeffrey had embarked on a low-voiced barrage of criticism.

Like a wasp, buzzing in her ear, Chellie thought wearily.

'Eloping with that con-man chap was bad enough,' he went on now, warming to his theme. 'But at least you had the excuse of infatuation. Yet now you brazenly admit you've also slept with this Brennan fellow—a man you hardly know. A virtual stranger. Have you no shame?'

'Yes,' Chellie said, lifting her chin. 'I am deeply ashamed that I didn't stand up to my father years ago, and that I ran away instead of confronting him. Will that do?'

'I see no call for flippancy.' He shook his head. 'I also realise that my sister was perfectly correct. All those lurid newspaper stories. She always said there was no smoke without fire.'

'Ah,' Chellie said, conjuring up an image of Elaine, all cashmere, pearls and disapproval. 'What a truly original thought—and worthy of the thinker.' She paused. 'Am I to take it that you've decided to withdraw from the proposed merger my father was trying to arrange?'

'I don't know what you're talking about.' There was faint defensiveness in his voice.

Chellie sighed. 'Yes, you do, Jeffrey. Isn't that why my father sent you to St Hilaire instead of coming himself? And why you agreed to come? Because he thought my ordeal would have cowed me into submission and I'd be ready to fling myself on to your waiting shoulder in grateful tears?'

His mouth tightened. 'I told your father that I was prepared to overlook your original indiscretion, yes.'

'So he dispatched you to kick me while I was down.' She smiled mirthlessly. 'He never misses a trick.'

'However, in view of your disturbing disclosures…'

'You've decided that I'd be more of a liability than an asset.' Chellie nodded. 'Very wise, Jeff. So there is light at the end of the tunnel after all.'

He glared at her. 'There may soon come a time, Michelle, when you will wish you hadn't dismissed me quite so lightly.'

'Jeffrey,' she said. 'As I've tried to explain before, more tactfully, I wouldn't have you if you came stuffed and garnished.'

'Charming.' His smile sneered at her. 'However, I don't think you've considered the full implications of your behaviour. There could be—consequences.'

'Possibly,' she said. 'But unlikely.'

'You seem to take the prospect of giving birth to an illegitimate child very lightly.'

'No,' she said. 'I'm just not prepared to waste time in fruitless conjecture. I'll deal with the situation if and when it happens.' *And I'll care as much as anyone could ever want,* she added silently.

She'd hoped that Jeffrey would be sufficiently offended to revert to sulking, but the damage to his pride was unfortunately outweighed by his sense of grievance. His complaints about her conduct jostled for position with dire prophecies for her future once his report to her father had been made.

'Understand this,' she interrupted him at last. 'I'm on this plane with you only because I'd already decided to return to England. It has nothing to do with any wish or decision of my father.'

'You'll toe his line,' he said. 'If you want food on the table and a roof over your head.'

'Other people earn their livings,' she returned. 'And so shall I.'

'Without any training or references? I don't think so. And none of the companies your father deals with would ever take you on, not if they knew it was against his wishes.'

'All the same,' she said. 'There are still places where his shadow doesn't fall. I'll make out.'

She turned away, pillowing her cheek on her hand and pretending to doze. But inwardly she was in turmoil.

Because there was more than a grain of truth in Jeffrey's unpleasant remarks.

The immediate future was bleak and frightening indeed. But the thought of surrendering meekly to her father's will was even worse.

I ran away once, she thought, but I'll never do that again. I'm not the same girl who thought someone like Ramon could possibly be the solution. I know now I have only myself to rely on.

There were tears, thick and acid in her throat, but she choked them back.

And Jeffrey had also been right when he described Ash as a virtual stranger to her, she realised bitterly.

On the surface he'd been Sir Galahad, rescuing her from danger. In reality he'd been Judas, selling her out for a lot more than thirty pieces of silver.

I should have realised he wasn't what he seemed, she thought, biting her lip. All the signs were there, but because I was attracted to him I didn't pick up on them. I let myself be fooled

After all, he knew exactly where to find me—and he broke into Mama Rita's desk—and knocked out Manuel. Not the usual skills of any passing stranger, even in Santo Martino.

And when I did ask questions he always had an answer. I see now why he hung on to my passport—to ensure that I didn't get away again.

But he did give it back to you, argued a small voice in her head. And he was planning to send you away from St Hilaire before the trap finally closed.

She stifled a sigh. He'd said he wanted to be with her, she thought desolately, but after all the deception he'd practised on her how could she believe another word he said?

The truth remained that all she knew was his name, and the fact that his lovemaking had driven her to the outermost limits of her soul. Not much on which to base an opinion, let alone the possibility of a relationship, she derided herself.

I allowed myself to dream, she thought soberly, and that shows how much growing up I still have to do.

For one thing, how seriously could she take his denial that he was seriously involved with Julie Howard? Quite apart from the picture beside his bed, there'd been real tenderness in his voice when he'd talked about her on board *La Belle Rêve*. And although he'd appeared shocked at the idea, the evidence was against him.

Besides, would he really be allowed to come and go as he pleased at Arcadie—invite anyone he chose to stay there in the owner's absence—if he was not regarded as already part of the family?

But she didn't have to make any kind of judgement on Ash Brennan or his romantic attachments, she told herself with resolution. Not any more. Because she was out of his life, and the distance between them was widening irrevocably with every minute that passed.

Even though that final image of him walking away from her was etched corrosively into her memory, hideous and inescapable.

Something else I need to deal with, she thought, her heart contracting painfully.

*　　*　　*

She maintained the illusion that she was asleep until they landed on Barbados. A car was waiting to whisk them from the airport to the Gold Beach Club Hotel where, Jeffrey had coldly informed her, they would be spending a single night, prior to the final stage of their journey back to Britain the following morning.

My last few hours in the lap of luxury, Chellie thought, as the car swung in between the hotel's tall wrought-iron gates.

The hotel was much as she'd imagined Arcadie would be, with the reception and public rooms located in a large low white-painted building, with cool marble floors, soft background music and air-conditioning.

The guests were accommodated in luxurious thatched bungalows nestling in the lavishly landscaped gardens, and there was not just one swimming pool, but three.

They were given a warm Bajan welcome, handed their keys, and told a porter would be along soon with their luggage.

As she turned away from the desk, Chellie found Jeffrey giving her one modest bag a beady look.

'Is that all you have?' he asked.

Chellie clicked her tongue reprovingly. 'Why, Jeffrey, have you only just noticed I'm travelling light?' she returned. 'How very remiss of you.'

'I have had other things on my mind,' he said repressively. He transferred the evil eye to what she was wearing. 'I suppose it's too much to hope that you have something to change into? They operate a dress code here.'

'I'm sure they do.' Chellie put firmly from her mind the thought of Ash's grey dress, neatly folded in the bottom of her bag. She would wear it some day, but it would certainly not be tonight.' She shrugged. 'But I'm afraid what you see is what you get.'

'Then I'll ask them to serve dinner in your bungalow.' Jeffrey pursed his lips. 'You'll be less conspicuous that way.'

'Really?' Chellie looked down at her tee shirt. 'For a minute I thought I had a large scarlet letter pinned to my chest.'

'Very amusing,' he said sourly.

'I wasn't joking,' she said. 'And I'm eating in the restaurant like everyone else. But I'll sit at a separate table if I'm an embarrassment to you,' she added coolly.

Jeffrey's face took on that unbecoming brick colour again, but he turned back to the desk and made a reservation for nine o clock. For two.

'Fine,' Chellie said briskly. 'Then I'll see you later—in the bar.' And she marched off with her waiting porter.

But once alone in her bungalow the bravado slid away. She stood, looking at her glamorous surroundings and the enticing view outside the window. The sound of voices and laughter, and the splashing from the pool area only served to deepen her sudden sense of isolation. And, if she was honest, the sniping match with Jeffrey had left her shaking inside, although a confrontation with her father would have been so much worse.

But how could Jeffrey have ever considered marrying me? she asked herself in bewilderment. My God, he doesn't even like me.

She had a long shower in the tiled bathroom, and hung up her skirt and top to try and get rid of some of the creases.

It's the dustbin for both of them as soon as I get back, she promised, wrapping herself in a dry towel, sarong-style, and stretching out on the bed.

She'd noticed a shop near Reception that sold beachwear, and there were vacant loungers round the pool, but she didn't feel like joining the party. There were too many couples about with eyes only for each other, and she felt raw enough as it was, with the reality of Ash's betrayal heavy in her mind.

But Jeff and I are going to stick out like sore thumbs in the restaurant tonight, she thought, her lips twisting in reluctant humour.

She turned on to her side, letting herself sink into the comfortable mattress. It was a huge bed—bigger than king-size—and certainly not designed for single occupation.

Which brought her back to Ash again, she thought, biting her lip.

Their lovemaking was disturbingly vivid in her mind. Her imagination exploded suddenly, creating an alternative reality where Ash lay beside her, his hands slowly unfastening the towel and slipping it from her body. Soft tendrils of desire were uncurling inside her, making her burn and melt, as she felt his lips possessing her inch by languorous inch, tracing a path from her throat to her breasts, then down over the flat plane of her stomach to the soft mound at the joining of her thighs.

She remembered the slow sensuality of his mouth exploring the sweet secret heat of her, the flame of his tongue bringing her to orgasm, and she lifted her hands and cupped her breasts, sighingly aware that her nipples were hardening irresistibly through the soft towelling.

She groaned, rolling over on to her stomach and burying her flushed face in the pillow.

'What am I doing to myself?' she muttered in anguish.

It wasn't even night and she was already out of control, aching for him, her newly awakened body crying out for the passion he had taught her and its surcease.

I must not recall those things, she thought. I must not remember the lover but the man who deceived me and sold me. The man I can never forgive. And certainly never, ever forget.

And then, at last, she allowed herself to weep for all that she had lost.

Jeffrey was already in the bar when Chellie, outwardly calm and composed, arrived there.

He was wearing cream linen slack trousers and a dark red shirt, with a cravat tucked into the neck, and drinking something through a straw from a hollowed-out coconut shell.

'So here you are.' There was something about the forced geniality in his tone and the faintly glassy expression in his eyes which led her to suspect that this wasn't the first coconut shell he'd encountered that evening, or even the second.

She said lightly, 'Full marks for observation, Jeffrey.'

But how many of me does he see, I wonder? she thought, climbing on to the stool beside him and ordering a sedate cocktail of tropical fruit juice.

When a waiter brought menus, Chellie ordered a Caesar salad, to be followed by red snapper. Jeffrey chose steak, and picked a bottle of red wine to go with it without bothering to ask if she had a preference.

I'll let him do the drinking for both of us tonight, Chellie thought with a mental shrug. Jeffrey Chilham with his hair down. Now, there's a thought to conjure with. And had to suppress a reluctant grin.

The restaurant was large and crowded with diners, the girls showing off their jewellery as well as their tans in skimpy designer dresses which left little to the imagination. A fact not lost on Jeffrey as the meal progressed.

'You'd look good in that,' he said thickly, as one beauty wandered past in an orchid-pink chiffon dress cut down to her navel.

'I know a woman called Mama Rita who'd probably agree with you,' Chellie returned, unsmilingly, as she drank some iced mineral water.

'Never heard of her.' Jeffrey refilled his glass. He paused. 'Not very talkative tonight, are you?'

'I have a lot to think about.'

'Wondering what lover-boy's up to, I dare say.' He smiled unpleasantly. 'Doesn't take much guesswork. His type have women waiting for them all round the world. He won't be lonely.'

'I'm more concerned with the future rather than the past,' Chellie said shortly, putting down her knife and fork. 'As I said, I have a living to earn when I get back.'

'Well, that shouldn't be a problem for a girl of your infinite talents.' He winked at her lasciviously over the top of his glass. 'Do what you do best, that's my advice. Once your hair's grown again you should be able to make a fortune on your back.'

Shock left her speechless. Mounting anger made her dangerous.

'Tell you what,' he went on, leaning confidentially across the table towards her. 'I wouldn't mind being your first customer.' He sent her an owlish grin. 'After all, you're bound to be feeling the lack tonight. You could probably do with some company.'

Chellie pushed back her chair and got up. She said quietly, 'I'll assume that it's the drink talking, shall I? And reply in kind.'

She walked round the table, picking up the bottle of red wine in passing, and poured the remains of it straight into his lap.

'You hellcat.' He was on his feet too, frantically dabbing at his soaked and stained trousers with his napkin as people at the surrounding tables stared and exchanged covert grins. 'Your father's going to hear about this.'

'Yes,' Chellie said crisply. 'He certainly is. And pretty soon, Jeffrey dear, you too will be looking for work.'

And she turned on her heel and walked out of the restaurant.

It was raining, Chellie realised with disgust as she emerged from the office block. There was a time when she'd have hailed a cab at once. Now, she dived into her bag for her umbrella, and started walking to the nearest bus stop.

There wasn't a bus in sight, which meant she was probably going to be late for her duty lunch with her father, she thought with a sigh.

It was a concession she'd acceded to with reluctance. And it had come at the end of a long and bitterly fought campaign to establish her independence. Which she seemed, incredibly, to have won.

It had been a difficult homecoming. Her father had greeted her with the ominous calm which invariably preceded a storm. And the storm had not been long in coming.

Clive Greer had wasted no sympathy on his errant child,

or the risks and dangers she'd endured. He'd dwelt instead
on her stupidity, her credulity, and her stubborn recklessness.

'Do you realise I've had to pay out a bloody fortune to
get you back in one piece?' he'd roared.

'Yes,' she said as pain slashed at her once again. 'I know.'

'And all to some soldier of fortune who doesn't know his
place.' He glared at her. 'Oh, yes, madam. Jeffrey felt obliged
to tell me what he'd discovered when he arrived—that you'd
lost all sense of decency.'

'Of course,' she said with irony. 'Your good and faithful
servant.'

'Not for much longer,' he retorted grimly. 'He's taking
early retirement for some damned reason. So I'm losing my
right hand, and I've got a daughter behaving like a tart with
every unscrupulous bastard who crosses her path. Pretty
good, eh?'

There wasn't too much she could say in her own defence,
so she bowed her head to the onslaught and conserved her
energy for the more important struggle to come.

The moment when she told her father that she was giving
up her flat and taking a room in a house with three other
girls who'd advertised for a fourth to share. And that, against
all the odds, she'd found a job as a receptionist and filing
clerk with a firm of accountants.

Sir Clive had resorted to his usual tactics, issuing com-
mands one moment, cajoling the next. Threats, Chellie
thought wryly, bribery—he'd tried them all.

Even emotional blackmail had been brought into play. 'I'm
not as young as I was,' he'd told her. 'And Jeffrey's decision
to leave has been a blow. I need your help, Michelle, your
support.'

'And I need a life of my own.' She'd remained rock-solid
throughout, steadfast in her determination not to be brow-
beaten or persuaded back into her old role.

'Then strike out on your own,' he'd shouted, angrier than
she'd ever known him. 'But you'll get nothing from me, so

don't come whingeing when you find yourself sleeping in a doorway.'

She'd not heard another word from him for almost a month, then he'd contacted her in person, instead of through his secretary.

Sounding oddly subdued, he'd asked if she would join him for lunch at his club.

She'd agreed to meet him against her own better judgement, afraid that he would start wheedling and manipulating, working to get her back into the fold.

Remembering how their previous battles had left her emotionally drained.

I can't start all that again, she thought. I *can't*—even if it does make me a wimp. But I've just managed to achieve some equilibrium, and I don't want to be thrown off balance again.

But the meal had gone better than she expected, probably because they'd adhered rigidly to strictly neutral topics of conversation.

All the same, she was sure that he was biding his time, circling round her, looking for a chink in her armour.

And he'd almost found it with Aynsbridge. She'd enjoyed being at the big Sussex country house more than anything else in her life, and when he'd mentioned almost casually that he was giving a small house party, and asked if she'd care to join it, she'd been tempted.

But then she'd seen it—the small, betraying gleam of triumph—and offered her regrets instead. He'd concealed his chagrin well, but she knew it wouldn't be his last attempt to make her dance to his tune, and that she needed to be wary.

He was sitting at his usual corner table, a buff envelope conspicuous on the white linen cloth. He rose as she approached.

'You're losing weight,' he commented abruptly as Chellie sat down.

'You're clearly not eating properly.'

'I'm fine,' she said. 'And I have three meals a day, including dinner. Everyone in the house has to take a turn in getting it ready, so some of the meals are pretty weird.'

He grunted, clearly uninterested in her domestic arrangements. 'You look pale, too.'

'My Caribbean tan didn't last long.' She kept her tone light, but wondered when she saw his mouth tighten and his fist clench on the envelope.

'So,' he said, as the soup was served. 'Still in that dead-end job?'

She smiled. 'It pays the rent—and for my singing lessons.'

His brows snapped together in the old thunderous way that used to frighten her. 'So you're still going on with that nonsense?'

'It's something I enjoy,' she returned composedly. 'And other people seem to enjoy it too. Jordan, who's teaching me, has managed to fix me up with a couple of gigs. I've actually been paid for them, too. And I'm singing at another tomorrow night,' she added. 'A private party. Someone's birthday.'

His frown deepened. 'Not using your own name, I hope?'

'I call myself Chellie,' she said. 'But I drop the Greer part.' She paused. 'Father—why do you hate it so much? My singing?'

He did not look at her. 'Because it took your mother away from me,' he said roughly at last. 'She was never—just my wife, as I wanted her to be.' He glared at her. 'Satisfied?'

She was silent for a moment. 'They say the more you let people go, the more willing they are to return to you.'

'What Christmas cracker did that come from?' Sir Clive asked with contempt. 'And who's come back to you lately? Not your gallant rescuer, I bet.'

She put her soup spoon down very carefully. 'No.'

'You won't either,' he said. 'I had him fired from that company he worked for. Told them I'd see them ruined if he stayed.' He paused. 'I dare say he wishes now he hadn't been so hasty, sending back his share of the money I paid them.' He smiled grimly. 'An expensive gesture, that, for someone who lives by his wits. It'll be a cold day in hell before he earns that much again.'

There was a sudden roaring in Chellie's ears, and she felt numb. She said, in a voice she hardly recognised, 'You're saying—Ash—sent back the money?'

'Yes.' He pushed the envelope towards her. 'It's all here in the report he submitted before he left, and the final statement from the company. He sent the cheque back himself.'

'Did he explain why?'

'Oh, there was a note with some arrogant comment about blood money. I tore it up.' He paused. 'Do you want to read the report? See what you cost me?'

She shook her head. Her voice was desperate. 'Father—the note—did—did it mention me?'

His eyes narrowed. 'No, and just as well. He's out of the company and out of your life too.'

'And that was your doing.' She closed her eyes, feeling sick. 'How could you?'

'I employed him to save you from the consequences of your own criminal foolishness.' Sir Clive's voice was harsh. 'Not to take advantage of the situation and seduce *my* daughter.'

Chellie stood up, trying to control her unsteady breathing. She said, 'I have news for you, Father. It was the other way round—I seduced him. And there hasn't been a day or a night since when I haven't missed him, or wanted him. And if he was here now, I'd tell him that I loved him.'

As she turned to leave, Sir Clive rose too. 'Where do you think you're going?'

'To find him,' she said. 'If it's not too late.'

'Then you're a fool.' The word cracked at her. 'And I've not time for fools, Michelle, so be warned. I forgave you once, but it won't happen again.

'Is this what you call having a life of your own?' her father demanded scornfully. 'Chasing a man who hasn't given you a second thought since you climbed out of his bed.'

'Oh, but you're wrong,'Chellie told him gently. 'He's given me much more than that. He's given me my life.'

She snatched up her coat, and was gone.

CHAPTER ELEVEN

'HERE are those earrings you wanted to borrow.' Jan wandered into Chellie's room after a perfunctory knock and paused, frowning. 'Hey, you're going to a party tonight, not a funeral. What's the matter?'

'I haven't had a very good day.' Chellie bit her lip. 'I've been trying to trace someone—an old friend—and so far I've had no luck at all.'

'The old friend being a man, of course?'

'Yes,' Chellie admitted. 'How did you know?'

'You've been crying.' Jan shrugged. 'It figures.'

'Oh, God, does it still show?' Chellie gave herself a distracted look in the mirror. 'I've been bathing my eyes too.'

'Well, don't worry about it.' Jan gave her shoulders a quick squeeze. 'Lorna's got some miracle eye-drops. You'll be fine.' She looked Chellie over. 'And that's a wonderful dress. I've never seen it before.'

'I've never worn it before.' The silvery material shimmered enticingly as she moved. 'But tonight I just—thought I would.'

'So who's giving this party?'

'A girl called Angela Westlake—or rather her parents. It's her twenty-first birthday, and they approached Jordan and asked if he'd play the piano during supper, and whether he knew anyone who would sing.'

Jan grinned at her. 'If you're not careful, honey, you could end up famous. Just remember who loaned you the earrings that got you your start,' she added as she went off to fetch the drops.

Left to herself again, Chellie applied blusher without enthusiasm, staring at herself with haunted eyes. She'd really

172

believed it would be so simple to find Ash. That it would take one phone call.

But when she'd finally screwed up the courage to ring the security company she'd been completely blanked by a frosty woman who'd told her they never revealed details about past or present employees.

Her only other hope was to telephone Arcadie. It was the nearest thing he had to a sanctuary, after all, she reminded herself. He might have gone to ground there while he considered his options. And while he licked his wounds too.

But the international operator had been unable to help either. St Hilaire had no listing for anyone called Howard.

So it was *impasse*, thought Chellie drearily. She couldn't afford to hire a private detective to find Ash, or go to the Caribbean and search for herself. Besides, she was unsure what she might find at Arcadie. There was still the unresolved question of Julie Howard, who might now have gained a new importance in his life. Or reasserted her former supremacy.

She might have leapt to the wrong conclusion about the money, too. Who said he'd returned it because of some feeling he still might have for her? Maybe—and more likely—it was simply Ash's way of drawing a line under an episode he now wished to forget. After all, their association hadn't done him much good, so perhaps he was clearing away the debris of the past.

And maybe it was wiser—healthier—for her to do the same.

She picked up her lipstick, put it down again, and closed her eyes.

If only, she thought, it could be that easy. But it wasn't. Ash was in her waking thoughts every hour of the day, and at night she tossed restlessly from side to side of the bed, consumed with longing. Burning up for him.

So she wasn't prepared to give up just yet. Not while there was an atom of hope—another avenue to pursue. And, of course, there was.

Laurent, she thought, her lips quivering into a smile. Laurent Massim. He and Ash sailed together, but they were also friends. He must know where Ash was.

And if he can't tell me, she thought, I'll know that Ash really doesn't want to be found. And, however hard it may be, I'll stop looking.

She looked at her watch. No time to call the operator this evening, of course. She had a party to attend, a professional engagement to fulfil. But tomorrow would be a different story.

She lifted her chin. I will do this, she told herself. It's not over yet.

The party was being held in a tall house in a leafy square. It was in full swing when they arrived. They were greeted by the hostess, a tall, attractive girl with a pleasant smile.

'Hi,' she said. 'So you're Jordan.' Chellie found herself being given a friendly but minute inspection. 'And you, of course, must be Chellie.' The smile widened. 'It's good to meet you. If you put your coats in the downstairs cloakroom, I'll show you where you'll be performing.'

They were taken down to a large basement room, covering almost all of the lower ground floor, where the supper was to be served.

A mouthwatering buffet was already laid out on long trestles, and there was a large tub filled with bottles of champagne on ice standing by. A number of small tables and chairs had been set out for the guests, most of them facing towards the baby grand piano at the other end of the room.

Jordan tried it softly with absorbed satisfaction as soon as Angela had excused herself and returned to her guests.

'The programme's been agreed,' he told Chellie. 'All stuff you know, that we've practised, and space for a couple of requests. I'm going to supply some background noise while the food's being served, then you come on.' He eyed her. 'You look different tonight—glowing, somehow.'

'It's the dress.' She did a half-twirl.

'No, it's more than that.' He paused. 'But put some of it in the performance. Don't hold back, Chellie. Show them what you're made of.'

'Don't I always?'

He shrugged. 'Sometimes I get the impression your heart and mind are elsewhere.'

'Ouch,' she said. 'Then tonight they'll get all of me. They'll have to if I'm to make myself heard over the sound of chewing,' she added cheerfully.

But, oddly, she found she did not have to compete with the chink of glasses and the scrape of cutlery after all. As she started to sing 'Out of My Dreams' from *Oklahoma*, a concert-hall hush fell on the room, and she was greeted with generous applause at the end.

She saw Angela Westlake standing at the side of the room, smiling and giving her the thumbs up.

'We usually do requests at the end,' Jordan announced. 'But we've been asked for a very special song right now— so, if it's all right with Chellie—here we go.'

Is he going to tell me what it is? Chellie thought resignedly as she smiled her acquiescence. Or am I supposed to guess?

Then she heard the opening chords and felt her heart jump crazily. Oh, no, she thought. Not this of all songs—please.

But the introduction was finishing, and there was nothing she could do but launch herself into the haunting first line of 'Someone to Watch Over Me'.

She was halfway through the first verse when she saw him, leaning in the doorway, almost unrecognisable in black tie and dinner jacket. Looking at her over the heads of other people as he'd done that other time. That first time.

Except there were no other people. The room might have been empty as she sang sweetly and wistfully for Ash alone, the slight huskiness in her voice adding poignancy to the words, an emotion that came straight from the heart. Holding his gaze with hers.

When she finished there was an almost startled silence, then the clapping began.

As she took a bow, instinctively her eyes sought Ash again, to see if he was joining in the applause—if he was smiling.

But Ash was turning away, walking to the door, pausing momentarily for a word with Angela Westlake and a swift kiss on the cheek.

Oh, God, Chellie thought frantically. He's going. He's leaving again, and if he does I'll never find him. I know it.

She turned to Jordan. 'I'm sorry,' she said. 'There's something I must do—someone I have to talk to.'

She threaded her way through the groups of guests, forcing herself to smile when a detaining hand touched her arm—to murmur her appreciation for the words of praise. When all she really wanted to do was run. Chase after him wherever he was heading.

He was nearly at the top of the stairs when she caught up with him. 'Ash—wait—please. Speak to me.' Her voice was desperate.

He turned slowly and looked down at her, the blue eyes grave. He said, 'You're wearing the dress.'

'Yes—something made me...' She swallowed. 'You don't mind?'

'How could I?' He smiled faintly. 'You look so beautiful you take my breath away.'

'In spite of my grotesque hair?'

'Maybe because of it.' He touched the silky strands, his fingers feather-gentle.

'But I wasn't asking for compliments. I want to talk...' She paused, her eyes searching his face. 'There are things to be said.'

'But maybe this isn't the right time,' Ash said quietly. 'Your audience will be missing you, songbird. You have them eating out of the palm of your hand.'

She swallowed. 'I wasn't singing for them. I was singing for you. You—must have known that. So why are you leaving? Because that's what you're doing—isn't it? You're going, and leaving me behind.'

'I must.' There was a raw note in his voice that she seized on.

'But why?'

He said gently, 'Chellie, your voice is going to take you to all kinds of places. I'd just get in the way. It's better that I go.'

She said with sudden fierceness, 'If that's how you feel, why did you give back the money?'

He stiffened. 'Who told you I'd done so?'

'My father—who else? He said you were a fool.'

'Yes,' he said. 'I'm sure he did. But I didn't expect him to tell you what I'd done. I thought he'd want to keep that a secret.'

'I'm sure he'll wish he had. Because you're not leaving without me. Never again.'

She lifted a hand, touched his cheek. 'He made you lose your job, Ash, and I'm so sorry. Because he'll probably stop you getting another one.' She bit her lip. 'You have no idea the kind of influence he has.'

'I got a good idea from seeing the effect he'd had on you,' Ash said grimly. He sat on the top step and pulled her down beside him. He said, 'Chellie, no one got me fired, least of all your father. I was already planning to go—it had all been arranged totally amicably, and then I was asked to do this one last job because it was my kind of thing.'

He shook his head. 'At first I said no, particularly when I found out what was involved. I had you down as some rich bitch who liked to live on the edge. My least favourite kind of person. But then your father started offering silly money, and I knew the business could do with a cash injection just then, so—for better or worse—I agreed.'

He sighed. 'I had all these strict rules for myself. Get the job done quickly, and no personal involvement—ever. And I tried my damnedest to stick to them—right up to the end.

'But with you, the ground was shifting under my feet,

and there were no bloody rules. I saw you, and I was lost. Caught up in this incredible, miraculous thing that I'd never really believed in. Knowing that I didn't have to be paid to keep you safe, because I'd lay down my life for you if necessary.'

He paused. 'All this I wanted to tell you, my beloved girl, and so much more. And then that dangerous buffoon showed up a day early and my chance went, and everything descended into chaos. I thought that I'd lost you for ever, that what we had was damaged beyond repair. You had every right to be hurt and angry about the way I'd tricked you, and any explanation I could give was only going to sound like some lame afterthought.

'Anyway, I told myself I'd blown it completely, and consequently nothing else seemed to matter. I made sure Victor got the money for the company, and then I—walked away.'

She said, her voice shaking, 'But that wasn't all of it, Ash. You had another reason to leave. There was Julie. You never really told me the truth about her, did you? And I have to know. Does she love you? Are you in love with her?'

'I should damned well hope not,' Ash said with asperity. 'Or my father will have me arrested. Julie's my young sister, and dying to meet you.'

She drew a deep breath. 'Your sister? Oh, I don't understand any of this. You said she was the owner's daughter. You had her photograph beside your bed.'

'Beside my father's bed, actually. He's the owner in question, and he can be a sentimental old devil, so there's usually one of me too. But I decided to put that particular piece of evidence away for the duration—in a very safe place—along with your passport,' he added, straight-faced. 'Just in case you started putting two and two together at some inconvenient moment. It didn't occur to me, however, you'd do exactly that and make five. Jools and I are fairly alike, if you look.'

'So Mr Howard—is your father?' She tried to unscramble

her thoughts as the joy inside her began to spread like wildfire through her veins.

'Mr Howard Brennan, yes. I can show you my birth certificate, if you want. And Julie's, too.'

'Oh, God,' she said on a little wail. 'Why didn't you tell me all this? Why didn't you explain at Arcadie?'

'Because in the kind of job I've been doing you keep personal details to a minimum. I learned that in the Army. You don't form relationships with the client. I was trying hard, against tough odds, to be disciplined, and stay away from you until the assignment was over.' His mouth twisted. 'And we both know what happened to that good intention.'

He took her hand. 'Anyway, darling, I thought you knew—that you'd guessed who I was and what I was about. Or some of it, at least. You said so.'

'I was talking about Julie.' Her fingers clung to his. 'I thought you and she were practically engaged,' she added with a little wail.

'And, that being the case, I was still trying to get you into bed?' Ash's tone was wry. 'You can't have a very high opinion of me.'

'I didn't know you. You'd done too good a job of keeping me at arm's length. I was just trying to make sense of it all, and failing miserably. I was so completely wretched I couldn't think straight.' She paused. 'And that's an explanation, not an excuse.'

She hesitated again. 'Tell me something now. Why did you come here tonight—if you meant to walk out again?'

He said with sudden harshness, 'I'm not even sure what I intended. I only knew that I needed to see you one more time. That I was gasping for you like air. But if you hadn't come after me, Chellie, I would have given you back your life and disappeared.'

'And I would have found you again,' she said. 'Some time—somehow.'

There was another round of applause from the basement, and Ash rose to his feet, pulling Chellie up with him.

'I think it's time we were on our way,' he said. 'Any moment Angie's gang are going to be pouring through here looking for the disco, the loos, or more drinks. They could trample right over us.'

'But I can't leave now,' Chellie protested. 'I'm supposed to be here to sing. I've got to see Jordan and explain—that's if he'll ever speak to me again.'

'He'll be fine. Angie's putting him straight at this moment.'

'The Westlakes are friends of yours?' She gulped. 'Of course. They would be.'

He grinned. 'Relatives, actually. Angie's mother and mine were first cousins, and pretty close. Why? Did you think I was gatecrashing?'

'I don't know what I thought. All I could see was you. All I could hear in my head was your name. It was like a miracle.'

Chellie paused suddenly, her eyes widening. 'Except it's nothing of the sort—is it? It's not even a coincidence,' she added on a note of breathless accusation. 'You arranged for me to be here. Ash Brennan—you set me up.'

'Just a little,' he admitted. 'Do you mind?'

'No,' she said. 'Considering I was going to call Laurent tomorrow and beg him to tell me where you were.'

'Oh, my love,' Ash said softly. 'My sweet love.' He paused. 'We could go back to your house, but I'd rather not run the gauntlet of the other girls yet. I need to have you strictly to myself.'

Chellie halted, staring at him. 'You even know where I live?'

He nodded ruefully. 'I asked Vic, my former partner, to keep an eye on you. We were in the Army together, you see, which is where we got the idea for the business, and we went through a lot together, so we've always been close.

'Besides, I was terrified you'd marry that idiot who came looking for you just to spite me,' he added, his mouth twisting. 'And I was hungry for any morsel of information about you—that you were well—that you were happy.'

'And what did he say?'

'Yes, to the first. Not very, to the second.'

'Well, he was right,' she said. 'And, after all, I have said more than once that I need someone to watch over me. So I can hardly complain when it happens.'

'I'm staying at a hotel temporarily,' he said. 'Will you come back there with me?'

'Anywhere,' she said. 'As long as we're together.'

'Oh, I can guarantee that,' Ash said. 'In fact I shall have serious trouble ever letting you out of my sight.'

'Then don't,' she said sedately, and went out with him into the night.

She'd expected a decent room—Ash was too fastidious for anything else—but not a penthouse suite in one of the capital's most prestigious hotels.

'Well?' Ash finished ordering champagne from Room Service and put the phone down.

'Very well.' She gave her surroundings another long look. 'Are you quite sure you gave back your share of the money?'

He shrugged. 'You had it straight from the horse's mouth. And you can always check my bank account later.'

'Later,' she said, 'has a nice sound.'

'Want to check the rest of the accommodation?'

The bed in the adjoining room was king-sized, and it was hard to notice anything else, but Chellie was determined to try.

'Heavens,' she said. 'How many channels on this television set?'

'I've no idea,' he said. 'And I have no plans to find out.'

Aware of his eyes following her, Chellie felt suddenly shy. She walked to the row of fitted closets and flung open a door. 'Oh.' She swallowed. 'You've brought rather more than a shirt and a pair of jeans this time.'

'I came prepared for a lengthy campaign.'

'You certainly did.' Her fingers slid along the rail and met silky fabric. 'And what's this?'

She just managed to catch the black dress as it slipped from its hanger. Turned to him with it spilling from her hands, her lips parting incredulously.

'You—took this?'

'I had to have something,' he said quietly. 'I didn't think you'd miss it. And it had some good memories for me.' He paused. 'Would you rather I threw it away?'

'Oh, no,' she said. 'In fact, I might even wear it again sometimes—birthdays—anniversaries—times like that. Create some more memories for both of us.' She let it drop to the floor. Unfastened the silver dress and sent it to join the pool of black at her feet. Stepped over both of them towards him.

She whispered, 'Darling—do we need champagne? I'm—really not thirsty.'

He stared at her, raw hunger in his eyes, harsh colour burning along his cheekbones.

He said huskily, 'But we might be—later.' And cancelled the order.

An hour had passed before Chellie stirred in his arms, her body sated, her heart full.

She said, 'So you weren't just a figment of my imagination after all. I did wonder.'

'I'm total reality,' Ash returned drowsily. 'Give me a few minutes, and I'll prove it to you all over again.'

She kissed his naked shoulder. 'Do you know, I was actually nervous? Isn't that ridiculous?'

'No,' he said. 'I was nervous too.'

'Under pressure?' There was a smile in her voice. 'What happened to the cheroots?'

'I've given up smoking. All part of the reformation. If I'm going to be a family man, I want to live to enjoy it.'

'Oh,' she said. She paused. 'Is that what you're planning?'

'It was,' he said slowly. 'But now I'm beginning to wonder all over again if I'm being very unfair.'

Chellie sat up and glared at him. 'You gave back a small fortune and went to all this trouble to find me—and you're having second thoughts?' She shook her head. 'I don't believe it. Unless you've decided you don't want me after all.'

'I hardly believe it myself, but I'm trying to be unselfish.' He looked into her eyes. 'Chellie, you have a God-given talent as a singer. I saw suddenly how they reacted to you this evening. You were tearing the heart out of them. And it made me think—how can I take her away from this? Is marriage to me any kind of fair exchange?'

He shook his head. 'Dear God, you've just escaped from your father. Do you really want to replace him with a husband before you've had time to breathe? What the hell have I got to offer in return?'

He took her face gently between his hands. 'I want you to have your chance, Chellie. The life you said you wanted.'

'You're the life I want.' She smiled back at him, her eyes warm and tender, a lump gathering in her throat. 'If you still want me. Singing is secondary. Although I suppose it could be handy as you're temporarily out of work. And spending everything you've got on expensive hotel suites and ladies to go with them.'

'Don't tell Dad I've no job,' he said. 'He thinks I'm his partner in his new brokerage and boat charter business, and is paying me accordingly. Why did you think I packed in the security game? I'd had enough of the high-risk activities and never staying anywhere more than a few days. I wanted a life too.'

He dropped a kiss on her hair. 'You see—you really were my last assignment.'

'So, where do we go from here?' She spread her fingers across his chest.

'How about a crash course in getting to know each

other—no secrets—no half-truths? Just the two of us, talking and loving. And alone.'

'It sounds perfect,' she said. 'What did you have in mind?'

'Dad's looking at this new boat and wants me to give it a trial in the Bahamas. I—I hoped you might come with me.'

She sighed happily. 'It sounds like heaven. And I've been learning to cook too.'

'I'm seriously impressed.' There was tender laughter in his voice. 'But I meant everything I said about your singing. I want you to be free to follow your star. It would be wrong to tie you down.'

'I could be a working wife,' she said. 'At least until the babies come. Then I can sing them lullabies.'

'Ah, darling,' he said. And found her mouth with his.

'We do have one remaining problem,' he resumed, some time later. 'Your father. He's not going to be happy about this.'

'The more you let people go, the more they want to come back to you,' Chellie said softly. 'He hasn't learned that yet, but I have hopes.'

'I have hopes too,' he said. 'And dreams. And you're at the centre of each one of them.'

She drew him down to her and kissed him.

'And we're going to make all our dreams come true, my love,' she whispered. 'You and I—together.' She smiled. 'And now you can order the champagne.'

But Ash's arms were already tightening round her. 'Later,' he said.

LIVE THE EMOTION

Modern Romance™
...seduction and
passion guaranteed

Tender Romance™
...love affairs that
last a lifetime

Medical Romance™
...medical drama
on the pulse

Historical Romance™
...rich, vivid and
passionate

Sensual Romance™
...sassy, sexy and
seductive

Blaze Romance™
...the temperature's
rising

27 new titles every month.

Live the emotion

MILLS & BOON®

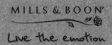

MILLS & BOON

Live the emotion

Modern Romance™

THE BANKER'S CONVENIENT WIFE by Lynne Graham

Italian-Swiss banker Roel Sabatino has amnesia and is feeling a little confused – he has a wife whom he cannot remember marrying! Hilary is pretty, sweet...and ordinary. But Roel still recognises a deal when he sees one and decides to enjoy all the pleasures marriage has to offer...

THE RODRIGUES PREGNANCY by Anne Mather

Olivia Mora didn't expect that one night of passion with handsome South American businessman Christian Rodrigues would lead to so much trouble! Determined to keep her pregnancy a secret, she retreats to a secluded tropical island. But Christian is a man who doesn't give up easily...

THE DESERT PRINCE'S MISTRESS by Sharon Kendrick

Multimillionaire Darian Wildman made an instant decision about Lara Black – he had to have her! Their attraction was scorching, and desire took over. Then Darian made a discovery that would change both their lives. He was the illegitimate heir to a desert kingdom – and a prince!

THE UNWILLING MISTRESS by Carole Mortimer

March Calendar is sexy, single – and she wants it to stay that way! Will Davenport might be the most eligible bachelor she has ever known, but he's also the most lethal. But from their first fiery meeting Will has been hooked on March – he wants her and will do anything to make her his...

On sale 5th March 2004

Available at most branches of WHSmith, Tesco, Martins, Borders, Eason, Sainsbury's and all good paperback bookshops.

0204/01a

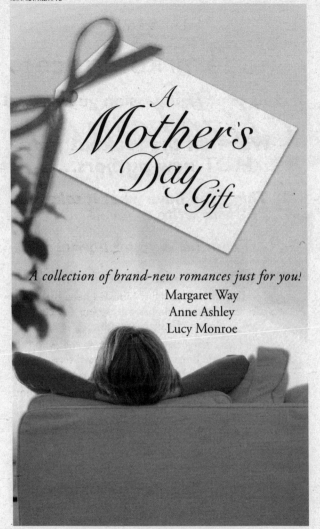

A Mother's Day *Gift*

A collection of brand-new romances just for you!

Margaret Way
Anne Ashley
Lucy Monroe

On sale 5th March 2004

Available at most branches of WHSmith, Tesco, Martins, Borders,
Eason, Sainsbury's and all good paperback bookshops.

FREE!

4 Books
and a surprise gift!

We would like to take this opportunity to thank you for reading this Mills & Boon® book by offering you the chance to take FOUR more specially selected titles from the Modern Romance™ series absolutely FREE! We're also making this offer to introduce you to the benefits of the Reader Service™—

★ FREE home delivery
★ FREE gifts and competitions
★ FREE monthly Newsletter
★ Books available before they're in the shops
★ Exclusive Reader Service discount

Accepting these FREE books and gift places you under no obligation to buy; you may cancel at any time, even after receiving your free shipment. Simply complete your details below and return the entire page to the address below. **You don't even need a stamp!**

YES! Please send me 4 free Modern Romance books and a surprise gift. I understand that unless you hear from me, I will receive 6 superb new titles every month for just £2.60 each, postage and packing free. I am under no obligation to purchase any books and may cancel my subscription at any time. The free books and gift will be mine to keep in any case.

P4ZEE

Ms/Mrs/Miss/Mr ....Initials..
BLOCK CAPITALS PLEASE

Surname..

Address..

....

....Postcode ....

Send this whole page to:
UK: The Reader Service, FREEPOST CN81, Croydon, CR9 3WZ
EIRE: The Reader Service, PO Box 4546, Kilcock, County Kildare (stamp required)

Offer not valid to current Reader Service subscribers to this series. We reserve the right to refuse an application and applicants must be aged 18 years or over. Only one application per household. Terms and prices subject to change without notice. Offer expires 30th May 2004. As a result of this application, you may receive offers from Harlequin Mills & Boon and other carefully selected companies. If you would prefer not to share in this opportunity please write to The Data Manager at the address above.

Mills & Boon® is a registered trademark owned by Harlequin Mills & Boon Limited.
Modern Romance™ is being used as a trademark.
The Reader Service™ is being used as a trademark.